Dis-Membered

A Murder Anthology

Clay —
Thanks for
Standing around :)

PUBLISHED BY:

The Authors of the Unblocked Writers Group

DISMEMBERED:

They Had it Coming

Cover Design by Annie Walls

All authors are members of the **Unblocked Writers Group** on facebook.

www.facebook.com/groups/244350892612/

This book contains graphic depictions of violence.

Acknowledgments

~~*

First, thanks to all who gave their time and effort on this project. Annie 'Kick Ass' Walls, once again, you came through with an amazing cover that really captured the spirit of what we wanted to do. Thank you so much! You are a force of nature and I am forever in your debt. Julie 'Jules' Watts, what can I say. You totally and completely rock. Thank you for making the time to edit, review and beta these stories. I couldn't have done this without you by my side. To Wayne DePriest, not only did you write a great story, you came up with a great title as well. To the founder of the 'Unblocked Writers Group', Tammy (tfc Parks). Through your vision, you've provided a home for a wild breed of misfit writers. Thank you for putting up with us.

To our victims—Josie, Rob, Annie, Atty Eve, Moira's parents, Woodrow Wilkins, Kris English, Beth Tully: Thank you for being such good sports. Your sacrifice is greatly appreciated and shall echo throughout the pages of history.

To the authors—Josette Weiss, C. Priest Brumley, Julie Watts, Rob Houglan, Vicki Barnes, Jessica M Kirkpatrick, Kris English, Annie Walls, Beth Tully, Wayne DePriest ... trust me when I say, it was a pleasure reading your stories and I appreciate the time you gave to this project. I look forward to working with all of you in the future and I wish you all the best in your writer lives.

Last, but certainly not least—our youngest writer, Moira Briggs. Let me just say I was completely blown away. To see someone so young with such an eye for detail is inspiring. And thanks to your mother (ED) for bringing you to our attention and giving us a chance to spotlight your talent.

You should all be proud of this project. I had a lot of fun and hopefully, we'll get to do this again.

 -Larey

Eulogy

~~*

Dearest friends, family members and honored guests, we are assembled here today to pay our final respects to the remains of an assorted bunch of characters, all who met their untimely (or timely) demise at the hands of the Unblocked Writers Group.

Whether by poisoning, decapitation, strangulation, repeated blows to the head, stabbing, un-elective surgery, fire, supernatural events, blunt trauma or a good old-fashioned ass-kicking, they have all served to remind us, in some small way, of just how precious the gift of life is to those they leave behind.

As for the perpetrators, it should come as no surprise, that the members of the Unblocked Writers Group are capable of committing such depraved acts. They are a special group. If you haven't met them, feel free to venture in to see for yourself. Just know, that a welcome wagon awaits, and it's filled with a collection of blood thirsty writers and the requisite tools of the trade.

So it is with somewhat heavy hearts, that we commit their latest batch of victims to the grave. Ashes to ashes, and all that good stuff. Break out the shovels and let's get this over with.

It's never easy to say goodbye to those we love, or like … or just tolerate. We know not what lies in wait for these dismembered souls. All we know, is that their number was up. Yet, as we mourn, we must also be reminded—that no matter how gruesome their fate …

...THEY

...HAD

...IT

...COMING.

One Shade

Of

Murder

Beth Tully

It's New Year's Eve 2028, and I'm preparing to attend the event of the year for the sexually adventurous in all of the Pacific Northwest, the HUMP Gala. I am not actually one of these, not from the Pacific Northwest and not all that sexually adventurous, but I have my own reasons for handing over $1000 for a ticket, and the same amount for an outfit that will fit in here.

I've chosen my look carefully, picking a designer dress that hugs my curves while managing to look as though I've borrowed it from my roommate, as if I'm the sort of girl more accustomed to wearing Converse sneakers. I pull a wig of heavy chestnut curls over my short blonde hair and give myself a quick burst of Bigger Lips from my Home Medi Spa robot. I've sawed a quarter inch off of the heel of my left shoe to give my gait an awkwardness that I know will arouse the predatory instinct in the man who is in fact my prey. My ass wiggles as I stumble through the parking garage in my building and go past my own spot, occupied by the red Mercedes I usually drive, and enter a small old purple Prius, a ridiculous car borrowed from an intern at the law firm where I work.

My timing is perfect. I pull up in front of the venue just as Jesus Gris and Maria Acero are pausing on the steps to pose for a photographer from The Stranger, the local independent newspaper that covers events like this and people like them. I wait until I am sure Jesus is looking at my joke of a car, wondering how anyone driving that thing could be at an event like this, before exiting and handing my keys to the valet, who looks confused at being presented with the keys to a car like this one.

I take in the frankly terrifying sight of the King and Queen of this prom for misfits. It has been 15 years since the world was obsessed with their vapid sexcapades and it had been 15 years before that the two of them had met and explored the world of S&M together. The years had taken a toll on both of them. Their eternal quest for youth, both in their own bodies and those of others, had led them to buy more and more evolved cosmetic surgery robots and the result had left them looking like surprised, indignant house cats with molded plastic bodies. They sought fresh flesh to satisfy Jesus's twisted sexual desires. Desires that Maria filled, briefly, in the widely read, if poorly-written series that was later made into a wildly successful softcore porn film.

That quest had led them to my sister, Claire. Writing this now, it seems like something dreamed up by a lonely, cat-hoarding Twilight fan, but my sweet sister had, just like Maria Acero, come to this city as a young, newly-graduated, twenty-one year old girl, not knowing what her future might bring. He'd found her working in a coffeehouse in the Capitol Hill district, and sent Maria in to befriend her and bring her under their spell. She accepted a job as Maria's personal assistant, not realizing what being alone with them every day would do to her. Before long, she wasn't just assisting Maria by getting her coffee and dry-cleaning, she was helping Maria in gratifying Jesus's fantasies as well.

All of that might have been fine, but Maria, seeing Jesus become more and more obsessed with this younger woman, wanted to recapture the heady times when the whole world wanted to read about Maria biting her lip. Her blog, which had dwindled to only a few thousand followers, started to get hits again when she intimated that they'd added a new girl to their sex play, and the attention from the internet public replaced the attention she was missing at home. She became more and more detailed and specific in her postings, and directed more and more vitriol towards my sister, Claire.

The comments section on Maria's blog became a dark and angry place where bitter lonely women made Claire the target of all their rage and frustration. Finally one day, Wanda Clemente, a small chubby woman with a mass of gray curls and watery, limpid blue eyes, used the information from Maria's blog to find my sister. She snuck into her house while she was at work, and replaced all of the artificial sweetener in her kitchen with rat poison. My sister was dead three days later. Wanda was caught and convicted, but Maria and Jesus's involvement in her downfall and eventual murder went unpunished. Tonight, I would end all that.

My car, and now my short skirt, had definitely captured Jesus's attention, and I felt his gaze on me as I passed them and entered the club.

Inside, the club had been transformed into a Sybarite's imagination. The dance floor was thronged with men and women of all ages, dressed in wisps of silk and satin. Above them, nearly-naked people of several genders danced on mirrored pedestals and, even higher than that, two completely naked girls swing and spin from trapezes that looked to be made completely of light. One had blue hair and one had red, and while neither of them had any pubic hair they had each painted a small strip of bright color where it would be.

I ordered a vodka soda from the open bar and positioned myself where I knew I'd be visible from the VIP dais where Maria and Jesus would be seated. The crowd parted before them as they entered and took their seats of honor. It only took another moment before Jesus saw me. He called one of the bouncers over and whispered in his ear, pointing at me. A moment later, the bouncer was in front of me.

"He wants you," the bouncer said, taking my agreement as a given. He led me to the velvet rope separating the two of them from the rest of the party goers, opened it, and gestured for me to join them.

I'd had most of this plan down cold, but I dreaded having to make conversation with the two of them. I was afraid Maria would say something unbearably stupid and I would not be able to control my desire to laugh in her smug, vapid face. Luckily, I'd no sooner settled myself on a

17

cushioned ottoman at their feet when the crowd on the dance floor erupted in a shriek.

Two of the naked trapeze artists had crashed, and high above the crowd their bodies bounced off of each other and became entwined in the trapeze wires. The one with blue hair dangled head down, one ankle wrapped in wire that she screamed was cutting into her flesh. "It's cutting my foot off!" she shrieked. "Help me!"

Everyone was looking at them. I'd never have a better chance.

I reached under my skirt and slid the two hypodermics filled with liquid cocaine out of their hiding place in my garter straps. Could I do it? After this, I would be a murderer. I might go to prison. Washington has the death penalty, even though no one has been executed here since 2021. Killing the two of them might be bad enough to bring it back. I had to steel my heart and think of Claire.

I removed the plastic cover from the needles, and held them in my hands, pointed towards them. Maria was wearing little more than a G-string, and her bare thighs looked soft and easily punctured. Jesus would be more difficult. His pants were a good-quality wool gabardine, but his shirt was a thin silk. I'd have to hit her thigh and his stomach at the same time. I imagined my arms at the correct angles. I could do this.

Claire wouldn't have wanted this. The thought hit me like a brick to the face. Like my sweet sister's spirit was speaking directly to me. This was wrong. It wasn't what she would have wanted. I should go home, take care of our parents. Not kill Jesus and Maria.

I let the tension slip from my body. All right, Claire. For you, I will let this go.

I started to rise from my ottoman, planning to find a trash can where I could dispose of my unused murder weapons.

"Wait," Jesus said, grabbing my wrist as I rose and throwing me off-balance. At that moment, three burly

18

firemen broke through the crowd and started carrying a ladder up to the VIP platform. One of them knocked into me and I fell forward. Instinctively, I put my hands out to break my fall.

My hands that contained the uncapped, cocaine-filled hypodermic needles.

I felt the palm of my left hand stop flat against the silk that covered Jesus's still rock-hard, if liposuctioned, abdomen. I felt my right grip Maria's bony thigh. I knew that meant the needles had found their mark. Both their bodies convulsed, but no one noticed as at that moment the trapeze wire sliced through the foot of the blue-haired trapeze artist, severing from her leg and sending her plunging into the crowd.

"Get out of the way," another fireman shouted, as they rushed to move a trampoline underneath the remaining girl. As they parted the crowd to move the inert body of the blue-haired girl away and try to rescue the redhead, I was pushed and shoved far from the VIP platform. I was, in fact, right by the exit. I stopped and rose up on tiptoes to peer at the VIP platform. Maria and Jesus were slumped over, but no one seemed to notice as the firemen unfurled the trampoline and the redheaded girl fell to safety. I slipped out the door and into the night.

~~*

19

Beth Tully is a Brooklyn writer. "I Should Hate You" is her unpublished memoir series which takes place in the punk rock scene of New York in the Eighties and early Nineties. It is the erotic, true story of an obsessive, doomed teenage love affair, shown through the prism of their sexual encounters as they explore, adore and finally degrade their own and each other's bodies."

You can follow Beth at:

http://www.writerscafe.org/writing/Mick_Lush/ 1027987/

https://www.facebook.com/BethTullyAuthor

Living Stiff

Annie Walls

Atty succeeded in opening her eyes from heaviness only to find she was shrouded in darkness. Memories flooded her mind as panic started an involuntary tremble in her body. The tarp that covered her felt like itchy canvas against her nose and forehead and smelled of freshly cut grass. Her mouth was gagged and her body bound to a table with thick straps. Numbness weighed her limbs down from the tightness.

The hopelessness of her situation began to weigh on her as questions came to her mind. *Where was she? What happened to her?* She remembered taking out the trash, but it got fuzzy from there. And more important, what was going to happen to her?

Letting out a scream, tears leaked down the apple of her cheeks in her attempts at struggling loose. She panted hard for air through duct tape, and thick saliva leaked from the openings as mucus flew from her nose, coating the tarp and her face.

"It's no use." The sudden voice made Atty pause in her battle. Her chest pumped up and down as she sucked in what little air she could through her nose. Swallowing a lump past her dry throat, she tried to pinpoint the location. Footsteps thudded closer and she was bathed in bright light. She blinked from the harshness of it. A man tossed the tarp aside. "Straps are quite tight." As to pinpoint the statement, the man thumbed the tension of one.

Once her eyes adjusted, a chill crept up her spine, locking her up with terror. The creak of small wheels drew her attention to what he was doing. An IV pole came into her line of sight. *What was he going to do with that?* It was not like she could ask. Her tongue felt heavy, and as panic set in, she jerked back and forth. The table rocked and screeched against the floor.

The strap at her torso jerked tighter, momentarily stealing her breath, but she continued her movements.

"I said it's no use." The stern tone did not match the smile on his face. The smile changed into something a little more sinister as his gaze left her face, roaming her body. "You have lovely skin," he murmured and seemed to force himself away. Atty noticed his thick accent. He was far from home, apparently. A weird hat adorned his head like some kind of joke. A witches hat, maybe, but Atty really expected it to open some eyes and tell her she'd be placed in Ravenclaw.

She felt a prick of a needle and watched as he set up an IV bag. A fog came over her and darkness blanketed her once again.

***

Scratch, scratch, scratch. The noise woke Atty up some time ago, and she could do nothing but listen to it. *Scratch, scratch, scratch.* Whatever it was, it didn't matter. She was no longer strapped down, but she couldn't move her body from the bed she was now in. Tubes snaked from her arms to the IV bag, no doubt keeping her groggy, too. Tears leaked from her eyes as she thought of her husband and children. She pushed those thoughts away and concentrated on the sound, hoping it would be like counting sheep.

She did not know how long she sat, counting. *Scratch, scratch, scratch.* A door opened and footsteps ensued. It was surely the next day. Day? *How long had she been here?* Her addled mind tried to take in her surroundings, but her vision blurred everything into a dreamlike scene. The footsteps stopped by her a brief second before continuing on. Another door opened on the other side and closed promptly. Straining past the beeping of machines, the footsteps faded as if walking down stairs.

For a moment, Atty was able to breathe a sigh of relief, but once again felt heavy as another dose of drugs made its way through her system.

Before she knew it, the door opened. The man had returned. "Ah, Atty. Time for a tour, shall we?" He was certainly chipper as he moved behind Atty's bed. The sudden jerk of the bed whirred as it lifted her stiff body into a sitting position and to her surprise it wheeled forward. She tried to speak but her mouth wouldn't work. A saliva-filled sound escaped her throat.

They didn't go far. She blinked as the man turned on a fluorescent light fixture—a buzz sound emanating from it. Her eyes widened at the collections of mannequins in front of her. They were posed and clothed in different ways. A pair sat at a table set up for tea, complete with princess china and plastic scones.

The man watched her with a keen eye. "You like them? I made them." Atty was not sure what she was supposed to think or do, not that she could, so she sat there like a log. A useless log. With a pursed expression, he took off the sorting hat to rub at his receding hairline. His gaze caught on her legs, and he dropped the hat behind her. Dropping to his knees, he picked up her leg—his gaze roamed the length. His hand soon followed. "Just like them," he whispered in a thick voice.

His eyes darkened. Dropping her leg with no care, he stood abruptly. Atty jerked from the astonishment of his sudden mood change.

He smoothed a hand down a mannequin leg. Foreboding zipped down her arms resulting in gooseflesh.

Atty's eyes caught the peepers of a mannequin after noticing, for the first time, the exact same IV tubes. The mannequin blinked and moaned. Atty screamed, but abruptly choked up as her stomach released thin bile onto her lap.

She woke up again to the feel of slick hands massaging her. Moaning, she watched as he rubbed a thick oil onto her naked body.

"Feels good, doesn't it?" He never looked into her eyes as his gaze followed his hands in only what Atty would call wonderment. Her stomach churned, but nothing ever came up. She supposed by the noise she made he figured it out. "Nausea medicine to keep you from vomiting again," he stated, meeting her gaze. Displeasure lurked in his eyes as he scrunched his face in revulsion. She supposed he didn't like cleaning puke. Atty couldn't describe what it was like to have him rubbing her most intimate parts only to come apart at his fingertips.

After he finished his game, he worked his way around the room for a while. Upon his return, he held up a bag from her bedside. He grinned as she caught sight of her bright yellow urine. He flicked her toe before changing out the bag. "Healthy woman. Your skin will be glowing in a week's time."

A week? Atty could not help the silent tears rolling down her face.

***

This became a routine of sorts. Weeks passed. She didn't know what time of day he came around, but when he wasn't, she'd listen to the persistent scratch and the muted moans of the mannequins. They were so soft, the sounds could be mistaken for wood settling.

Her body grew a body clock around the man. When it was time, the man came in and went straight to the door, going down the stairs. Atty supposed it was a supply closet, or maybe more mannequins, she didn't know. One time she heard quite a commotion of metallic banging, and the man screaming with rage that vibrated the floor beneath her. It took some time for him to come back up, but when he did, he acted as if nothing had happened.

What she did know was her fate would be the same of the mannequins. She hoped to deter him with her moans of pleasure and her eyes, but he never relented to her wiles and still seemed gratified in her responses. After he finished moisturizing her skin, he'd all but worship her and bring her to a peak—sometimes quickly, but other times more slow and teasing. She found herself resenting and looking forward to it at the same time. Then he'd move her

28

to a sitting position and go around the room for a time changing catheter and IV bags.

Even as she grew fond of his veneration, she also started to know the noises of the mannequins and what they meant. This was a strange feeling, almost like they had a language of their own. It grew comforting in the times the man wasn't there.

It came to be that time was irrelevant. Atty supposed this was what the man wanted, and as long as he was pleased, she was content for the time being. Atty knew he wouldn't kill her. He hadn't hurt her in anyway, hadn't raped her, and in a sense treated her as if his queen. The only thing that mattered was keeping the man happy while she waited for an opening of some kind. Yes, the little bit of hope was still there, especially at times when the faces of her family flipped through her mind.

Then everything changed. One day the man came in and set up video equipment. Sounds came from the mannequins all at once as if they knew what was coming. They were muffled sounds of contained excitement. Her lower regions clenched and grew warm in anticipation.

Her stomach and heart plummeted when the man completely ignored her. Not even looking at her. Not one word of admiration. She gave out a sound of dissatisfaction at the abrupt change in schedule, but when he didn't respond, she quieted down to wait. He'd get to her eventually.

She watched as he had tea with the tea party, talking to them in a one-sided conversation, but paused as if they were speaking back to him. He turned on music and danced with the standing mannequins that stood on rolling stands, whispering in their ears as if they were lovers. He'd chuckle seductively as if they whispered something naughty and funny at the same time. Holding a camera, he recorded them as he brought them all to peak one by one while Atty watched with open fury and agony.

After a time, he paused and gazed lovingly at Atty. "You'll be the best yet."

After his praise, a series of groans ensued. Atty soared to a new height she didn't think possible of this situation, even though he did not come near her. He smiled at her and returned his attention to the other mannequins.

With revelation, Atty realized the women trapped in this hell loved his attention and couldn't bear having him admire her. Her stomach churned and she convinced herself she would not come to love him, but from her own reactions, maybe she already did. She couldn't believe it. No. Not possible. She was only trying to find a way to escape, wasn't she? Biding her time?

With certain apprehension and despair, she watched them for hours. He finally drew near, only to change her bags and leave.

***

The next day, after a long night of silence with the exception of the scratch, which she now believed was a rat, the man was attentive to her and only her.

"I believe you're ready, Atty." The mannequins let out soft wails almost like mockery. "Shh!" he hushed them. "She'll be better than you all." Even her heart constricted at the scorn. With that statement, he wheeled in a massive stainless pot. Steam rose from the contents. The man fiddled with her IVs, and she felt a huge fog pull her over. He began to arrange her legs as if she was sitting and placed two-by-fours underneath her like a chair. He then moved one of her arms—one behind her neck, the other placed across her stomach.

Of course, she could do nothing as he paced, his gaze never leaving the positioning of her limbs. He stopped and blew out a breath, "This is going to be a challenge. I'll need to save that arm for last."

He sat on his wheeled stool, wiggling his fingers in latex gloves. She felt herself cringe at the snap they made on his wrists. "This will be warm, but I promise to make you as comfortable as possible." His gloved hand caressed her bent knees. "The first coat will be the worst."

She stared at the ceiling as he rubbed hot liquid into her skin, starting at her feet. It was more like a scrubbing motion. Thick saliva caught in her throat like a bubble as tears streamed from her eyes. It was happening and there wasn't anything she could do about it.

After a few hours, he was at her thighs when the fog began to lift and she could feel the tautness of her skin on her toes, feet, and calves. The stiffness grew worse by the minute almost crawling up her knees and thighs as the concoction dried. Her breathing picked up and came out in harsh pants as her pulse pounded in her ears. It took the man a few moments, but he noticed, rolling to the IV machine. In a second, her lids grew heavy and nothing.

***

Atty woke to harsh sobbing. Now, she was in a standing position and could look about the whole room without moving her head. She supposed he did this on purpose. Her body felt as if contained in a thick body cast, but the look of her skin glowed with a sheen. Just like the mannequins. She was wrapped around a pole of some type. The sobbing grew louder and she found the man on his knees in front of the tea party. His face was in the lap of a mannequin as his shoulders wracked his entire body. Mournful sounds came from the others. Atty herself felt mournful as she watched the man in his grief.

Days came to pass and the man seemed lost. He did nothing but change bags once a day, give Atty another coat of clear wax and leave again. No going downstairs. No words. No admiration. No pleasure. His eyes were in a faraway place. Atty's body ached, not only from the newness of her stiff posture, but from the lack of attention she'd grown used to. Only one thing remained the same—that goddamned rat.

Atty was in a state of nothing. Nothing remained. Not one shred of hope. Not even hope of attention from the man as he came and went—until a screeching noise brought her attention to the downstairs door. It crashed open, and Atty could not believe what she was seeing. The others made noises of astonishment as well.

A woman stood there. Frozen, wide-eyed, gagged—deranged. Her long, dark hair was nothing but a tuff of tangles. She bled from her red wrists. Filth covered her feet and clothing—a yellow sundress that hung from her bones. Bruises marred her sunken cheeks and kneecaps that shook as the young woman took in the scene before her. Finally, the woman unbuckled the gag around her face. It dropped to the floor as she neared the closest mannequin, which happened to be Atty. The woman's trembling hand reached out and touched Atty's arm secured around the pole. Atty groaned, and the woman jumped back.

"Shit!" Her voice was hoarse. Resentment flowed through Atty. *The man kept this woman? What was he doing with her? How long was she down there?* And now that Atty thought about it, the man hadn't been to see her in days. Atty stared at the preconceived rat and wanted nothing more than to throttle her as jealousy took over her emotions.

Upon gazing at the other mannequins, the woman moved into action. One by one, looking at them all closely. She stopped at the dead one, bending to have a closer look. When she reached out to touch it, the plastic arm holding its position gave way and the mannequin fell forward. The woman startled backwards, wrapping her hand over her nose and mouth as if she could smell the death. The woman gagged, throwing up yellow fluid.

32

An enraged sound filled the air, coming from somewhere near. Atty watched as the woman panicked, looking around. Atty's own heart was in her throat, threatening to bust out of the casing she was enclosed in.

The woman rummaged through drawers quickly as heavy stomps came closer to the outer door. She hunched behind where the door would open in a squat. The door slammed open, momentarily stealing Atty's view of the woman. The man looked around. His gaze took in the open downstairs door, the fallen mannequin and then the rest of them.

"Annnnie ... You're not where you're supposed to be," he said, talking calmly, but emotion brought out his accent thicker. "You'll have to forgive me for being neglectful. You hungry?" His tone was consoling and regretful. Atty knew she'd do whatever he wanted if she was the woman.

He took a tentative step forward, and the woman dove at his feet slashing at him. Blood spurted from the backs of his ankles. He cried out, falling to the floor. The woman didn't waste time, pouncing, rolling him over and straddling him. She grabbed his throat with one hand and raised the other. Atty noticed a scalpel in it and let out a sound of agony even as a bit of satisfaction flowed through her.

The man let out a choke and grabbed at the woman—grabbing her face, her hair, but she ignored it. She slashed down one arm and then the other, but his flailing made her attempts harder. Eventually, his arms rendered useless at his sides—sliced up—as blood pooled around them both. The man grew weak with blood loss and the woman tossed the scalpel, wrapping both her hands around his neck. Tears of sorrow streamed down Atty's face, even though she could not feel them. With a purple face, the man gagged for air. The woman hocked a spit into his face and let him take a ragged breath, bringing a little color back into his face. Then her shoulder blades shifted as she put more

33

pressure on his air passage. As the man let out a silent open-mouthed gag, the woman laughed and leaned back a little. He coughed, "Please."

The woman cackled again. "Go to hell." Her hands grabbed his neck, and the next sound that burst from him was his last.

Silence became thick in the room before muffled sobs came from the mannequins, including Atty. The woman stayed straddled across the man, staring down at him as if to commit the sight to memory.

After an eternity, she stood, glancing around the room in a shock-like state. She walked out and Atty could only hope help was coming.

She waited.

They waited in quiet.

Minutes passed. A half hour. Then she smelled it—smoke. It started to fill the room rapidly as flames licked inside the doorway at the ceiling.

Atty knew what was coming. She could only hope the wax didn't prolong the pain she would endure. As more tears leaked from her eyes, she knew she was going to hell right along with him.

~~*

Author of dark fantasy and sub-genres of horror. Voracious Reader and Googler. Lover of Dark Humor. Horror Buff. Zombie Apocalypse Enthusiast. Amateur Photographer and Graphic Designer. Artist. Cake baker and decorator. Earning a BA in English concentrating in writing. Mommy. Wife. Friend. Well, yeah, I'm one crafty bitch.

You can follow Annie at:

www.anniewalls.com

https://twitter.com/TheAnnieWalls

https://www.facebook.com/pages/Annie-Walls/106813269482996

Sing Me the Blues

Julie Watts

How did we get to this place? Anabelle wondered as she sprinkled the crystals, sifting them through her fingertips, so they evenly covered the pizza slice—Papa John's, double bacon and cheese pizza, with onions and roma tomatoes. Woody's favorite. She loved Woody, loved him enough to do this.

Standing at the sink, she scrubbed her hands, washing away all traces of the poison. She let the warm water run over her fingers, arthritic fingers that only yesterday fumbled with her front door key while the phone inside rang …

~*~

As she tried to insert the key into the lock, the phone rang for the third time. Darn that Woody, if he would just give a little. She watched other people on their cell phones, taking calls, anywhere and everywhere. He didn't even want an answering machine. He said he liked his privacy. Finally, the key slipped in and she twisted the lock open, just as the phone finished the fifth ring. Most people didn't wait beyond six rings, and the thought made her hurry just a little, not bothering to remove her snow boots, before trudging down the hall. She picked up just before the eighth ring, hoping 'whoever it was' would still be there.

"Hello." It came out in a rush. She half listened to the voice at the other end as a hot flash kicked in full force and she worked at the buttons of her coat with gloved fingers. "Yes, Doctor Cummings, this is Annabelle. " Unable to get the first button undone, she dropped her purse to the floor and pulled off the gloves. "Yes, I'm here," she settled the handset between her ear and shoulder as she worked at the buttons. "Yes, I've been anxious about the test results since I saw you … They were all ok? Just menopause?" … *Only a man could refer to it as 'just menopause'*, she thought, as she pulled the coat open. "But, it's been going on for four years now… Yes, that's a relief, I was sure it was something more serious." Her voice warmed a little as some of the tension left it. "Thank you so much for calling."

She started back down the entry, hoping to get her boots off before she made too big of mess from the clinging snow. After three

39

steps, she sighed and turned back to answer the phone a second time. "Hello? Yes, this is Annabelle, Woodrow's wife. Oh, hello, Doctor Hornbeck. I'm sorry, Woody's still at the station. Were you calling about the results of his last tests?" She picked up her gloves from the table and fanned herself. "Has the chemo done any good?" She stopped fanning. "I see," the corners of her mouth drooped as her face paled and went slack. "I see... yes, I understand. You went over that possibility when we were there. And there is no chance ... no chance of a mistake?" She dropped down onto the edge of the chair and slumped against the back. "I see ... yes, if you'd like to call back later and discuss this with Woody, I'm sure he'd appreciate it. Thank you. Yes, goodbye." Annabelle missed twice before she got the handset back into place.

She was still sitting by the phone, when she heard the jingle of Woody's keys, and the sound of the front door opening. Straightening up in the chair, she wiped at her eyes and sucked air deep into her lungs. She tried to smile, but the result was not convincing.

"Hey, Sugar." Woody strolled up the hall, slowing as he neared. "Annabelle, what's wrong?"

"Wrong?" she asked, then followed his gaze to her boots. They were swimming in a puddle of melted snow. "Oh, dear. I ran in to catch the phone. The doctor called ..."

"What did he say?"

Tears welled in her eyes. "Oh, Woody. It's not good."

He supported himself with a hand on the table, his knees creaking as he knelt beside her. "Ah, my sweet Annabelle." He pulled her against him and held her tight. "We'll get through this. We always do, don't we?" Placing a finger under her chin, he lifted her face to his, leaning a little to look into her eyes. I love you, baby. I always have, always will." He stroked her cheek with his thumb. "No matter what."

"I know," she sniffed and tried to smile as she caressed his lips with her fingertip.

Woodrow covered her hand and kissed her finger. "Now, why don't you go take off those boots. I'll get the mop."

~*~

They avoided the subject for the rest of the evening, doing what they did, what they always had—concentrated on making life good for the other. That was how they had survived lost jobs, six children and forty years of marriage. They finished off one bottle of wine and opened another. Then Woody turned the stereo on low. He picked up her hand and guided her to the center of the room, where they danced. It was a night for the blues. Afterward they made love. Slowly. Sweet, gentle love.

"Woody?" Annabelle lay snuggled against him, her head resting on his chest, his arms tight around her.

"Hmmm?"

"You remember talking about what our wishes were if ever ... well, if we ever found out we had a terminal illness, or wouldn't recover from a terrible accident?"

His arms grew tighter. "Yes."

"Well, I just wanted to make sure that, well... you know... we still want the same thing."

"Annabelle, I don't want to live as a vegetable, or in terrible pain. If it ever comes to that point, and I can't do it myself, I want you to put me out of my misery. That's why we bought that concoction, just in case. I haven't changed my mind." He kissed the top of her head and rubbed her shoulder. "How about you? Have you changed your mind?"

"No," she answered quietly. "I haven't changed my mind." Annabelle fought back tears, trying to be brave. She would have to find strength somewhere, from deep within. Woody's arms loosened as his breathing deepened. She rolled onto her back, threw off the covers and fanned herself.

~*~

"Annabelle, do I smell double bacon and cheese?" Woody peeked around the kitchen door.

"Yes, I thought we'd have something special tonight," she tried to smile.

41

He kissed her cheek and went to the wine cabinet. "I guess we'll need some wine, maybe some red zin?" He asked as he pulled out two wine glasses.

"My favorite."

Annabelle looked at the pizza on his plate as she carried it to the table. No sign of the poison. *No pain, no agony*, the man had said. *It will take a few hours to take effect and, basically, you just fade away in your sleep.*

Woody placed a half-filled glass near each plate and they sat down to eat. *Our last meal together.* Just as they were ready to begin, the phone rang.

Annabelle started to rise to answer it. "Leave it," Woody said. "They'll call back if it's important."

"But, it might be important. It might be your doctor calling back to talk to you." The phone continued to ring.

"What do you mean, calling back? I thought it was your doctor who called."

"He did. Rather, they both did." The phone rang again.

"What exactly did he say?"

"Doctor Cummings said it's 'just menopause'. Doctor Hornbeck said that, well ... your chemo didn't work. He was going to call back to talk to you more about it. That might be him." The phone stopped ringing in the middle of the fifth ring.

"What else did he say, Annabelle?"

"He said there was nothing else they could do." Her voice cracked and tears filled her eyes as she reached for her wine.

"Wait, Annabelle." He reached for her hand, as she brought the glass up. "Wait." They lowered the glass together and his hand stayed there, on hers. "So it isn't you, it's me? I thought when we were talking last night... that it was you ... But..." He looked down at his plate and back up, searching her eyes. "The pizza?"

She nodded, tears now cascading over her pale cheeks.

"Ah. I see."

"This is what you want? You're sure?" She whispered.

"Yes." He smiled at her. "Annabelle, let me have your wine."

"My wine?" She hesitated before pulling her hand back from the stem. "I see."

42

Woodrow picked up her glass, lifted it to his lips, tipped his head back and drank. "Ah," his eyes twinkled. "A very good year." Rising, he held out his hand. "Annie, come here."

Annabelle rose, and he pulled her to him, her arms snaking around Woody's neck as he held her close. One large hand moved softly down her side to settle at the smooth curve of her hip.

"Sing me the blues," she whispered.

Woodrow's deep voice was muffled as he sang, his lips pressed against her fragrant hair. And they danced.

~~*

Julie Watts is fully committed to her attention deficit, hyperactive personality. Her past writing includes articles published in Nebraskaland magazine; the poem, THREE HAPPY WIDOWS, published in Ellery Queen Mystery Magazine; and a musical, THE CAST, performed on stage by The Sheridan County Players. While she lives in Nebraska, she works in South Dakota, Wyoming and Nebraska, caring for our Veterans. Around work, family and building a cabin in the Black Hills, she manages to dabble in photography, music and new writing projects, but is waiting for retirement to finish those five books that reside in her files.

Memory Details Assignment

C. Priest Brumley

"With rare exception, one can not write on a subject unless one experiences it first. This is a cardinal rule of writing. Tragedy, sadness, happiness; every experience you have marks you, it stays with you in some form or fashion throughout your life."

"The more powerful of the memories, of course, stay longer, occurring frequently within the mind's eye. The details of the event; the rough-hewn edge of a man's shirt, the scent of a woman's perfume, all stay, ready to be recalled at a moment's notice, with or without provocation."

Professor Wayne DePriest, head of the English department at East Jefferson High School, took a moment to stare at the sea of faces around him. "The applications for this lesson, of course, are broad, spanning almost every discipline of writing you can ima—"

The bell tolled in the distance, a shrill pierce cutting Professor DePriest off at mid-sentence. "We'll resume this thread tomorrow. Homework: write a short piece describing an event from your past in as much clarity and detail as you can. Editing is not necessary. Try to keep under a thousand words. And it's due Monday, so you'll have the whole weekend to do it, okay? Go on."

The class rose in fits, filing from the room in the spurts that showed the true segregation of youth: the achievers left first, anxious to begin their next challenge, fiending as addicts for the drug of knowledge. The next were the middling crowd, the many who merely hoped to end their day without falling adrift of the losing side of the grades battle. Then came the lolly-gaggers, as Professor DePriest liked to call them. The slackers, the sleepers, and the inattentives who worked tirelessly to undermine his teachings without working at all. These were the students he tried to reach more than anything, the gems secreted away under the mountains of laziness. If he could bring just one of them out of their shell and inspire them to showcase their true talent, he had done his job properly.

"Umm, Mister DePriest?" It was Kristopher, one of the newer faces on the year, a brilliant kid with an aptitude for writing that had, at times, impressed the man now standing over his desk.

"Whatcha got, Kris?" With the class gone, Wayne had removed all pretense and authority from his voice. It was a tactic he'd found to work well over the years in dealing with the lolly-gaggers, making them feel as though he was talking *to* them, rather than *at* them.

"Well, you said to write a piece about something that's happened to us in the past, right?"

"Indeed I did. What's the question?"

"What if I wanted to write something about a *new* experience, something I'm going to do? Would that count?"

Wayne felt his hand stroke the edges of his salt-and-pepper moustache as he considered the proper answer. "I don't see why not. After all, the recent past is still the past, wouldn't you say?" Kristopher's enthusiastic nod was all the prompt he needed to continue. "However, since I know you're capable of it, I'll tack a little something on to the assignment, should you choose to accept. If you do it, you get bonus points toward your overall grade. If not, well, no harm, no foul, as they say."

"Okay. What is it?"

"I want you to write about a murder." Wayne watched with mild amusement as Kristopher's eyes grew wide with shock. "I don't want you go out and kill anyone, Kris. So here's the kick: you have to do it using your imagination. Draw on your memories and experience for what you can, but for the kill itself, you have to imagine up every detail you can muster. Sound doable?"

Wayne watched as Kristopher struggled to find an answer.

"But, the assignment—"

"—Is for everyone else. I know you're a good writer, kid. Some of your stuff this year has been flat-out brilliant. The Sonnet assignment? Stone-cold brilliant, if I do say so

48

myself. And now, I'm presenting you with a challenge. If you don't want to do it or don't feel as though you can, it's okay. I just thought you would like the extra challenge."

The teenager's face lit up at the praise. "So you want me to write a murder scene, using as many details from memories and life experiences as I can while imagining the murder itself in detail, am I right?"

"Right."

"Can-do, sir! See ya Monday!" Wayne's smirk followed the squeak of Kristopher's high-tops out of the classroom.

* * * * * *

The following week had been a flurry of activity, with the staff's Christmas party and school rally and Wayne's family coming in to town for the holidays. Grading had always been the thing to fall behind in any situation, this time proving not to be the exception. Those of the class that had turned in stories waited the last week before the holiday break for news of their grades, all to no avail. Wayne decidedly kept to the lesson plan for the last week, allowing the Friday before the break for his classes to goof off and blow off some steam.

A bell tolled in the distance. The winter break was here at long, blessed last.

Wayne stooped to the locked drawer at the bottom of his desk, retrieving the small pull-along he had carried his books in for the last ten years. When he emerged, Kristopher was standing at his desk, backpack dangling from one shoulder, looking all the more like a child facing the gallows.

"Everything okay, Kris?"

"Yes sir. Umm, I was just wondering if you'd read the story I handed in yet?"

Wayne felt a pang of guilt clench his stomach. With everything that had happened in the time intervening, he had forgotten the extra assignment entirely. "Not yet. I, uh, planned to read through the stories over Christmas break. It'll give me more time to grade them appropriately. Sound fair to you?"

"Yes sir. I was just wonderin'. Have a Merry Christmas." And with a squeak of tennis shoes, Kristopher turned to the classroom door and made his exit. Wayne felt the knot of guilt ease a bit, and, retrieving his fedora from the next drawer up, made his way to the faculty parking lot.

It was an hour later on the drive home that the call came. Fumbling for the cell phone lodged firmly in his pants pocket, Wayne managed to slide the "answer" bar just in time to avoid missing the call altogether.

"Hello?"

"Yes, is this a Mister Wayne DePriest?" The voice was female, with a husky edge and a hint of a northern accent.

"It is. To whom am I speaking?"

"This is Lieutenant Parks from the Jefferson Parish Sheriff's Office. Do you have a moment to speak?"

"Indeed I do. Can I help you with anything, ma'am?"

The sound of shuffling papers hit his ears before her voice came back. "Yes. We're trying to find a student of yours, a Kristopher Bates? We were told that he's in your final class of the day, so you're possibly the last person to see him. Do you have any idea of where he might be? Maybe where he might have gone after school?"

"No ma'am. He stayed behind to ask about a writing assignment he'd turned in and then left. I didn't see where he was going at all."

"Ah." Lieutenant Parks' disappointment was palpable through the receiver.

"If I may ask, why d'you need him? He's always seemed like a good kid to me. Never late, bright as a bulb—"

"He's a murder suspect."

Wayne didn't see the car stopped in front of him until it was too late.

* * * * * *

His hospital stay lasted all of a day. Doctor Delph managed to cast his leg as well as she could, with the remaining time set aside for rest. On her orders he stayed in bed for the next week, foot raised on a stack of precariously balanced pillows. When time came for Christmas Day, he managed to monopolize the entire sofa, an act eliciting mutinous grumbles from the gathered family members.

After Christmas, the time came to get back to work.

* * * * * *

The desk lamp felt hot on Wayne's hands as he sat through the night in his study, with one week left to go before the start of the second semester. The stories were primarily anecdotes of teenaged life, recollections of bitchin' parties and first kisses (names removed for fear of repercussion, of course). Wayne sped through the majority of them, giving points where he saw fit, "A"s for those who had taken the time to ensure proper grammar, "B"s for those who hadn't, and so on.

At long last, and with a rather harsh jolt, he came across Kristopher's submission. It was towards the bottom of the stack, two sheets of loose-leaf paper bound by a single staple, cramped handwriting in black ink covering the fronts and backs of both pages.

Wayne felt his fear bubble up, the acrid stench of stomach acid mingling with the battery-copper taste in his mouth, felt the slight tremble of his aged hand as he lifted the sheaf and began to read:

Memory Details Assignment

By Kristopher Bates

"I creep along the hallway, as silent as a mouse. The carpet masks the sound of my footsteps, one foot in front of the other, as I make my way to the door at the end of the hall. I can hear the snoring, which means she's asleep.

Good. All for the better, I suppose.

As I peak my head around the doorframe, I see her laying in the bed, as elegent as a swan. The pale white nightie barely covers her ~~tits~~ breasts, pale half-orbs of perfection, moving up and down in a slow rythem. I feel a stir in me, but I quiet my feelings so I can do what needed to be done.

The knife is in my hand, hard plastic handle slippery from sweat. I feel my arm rise, then

fall, and I hear the wind
rustling the curtain, and I know
I have to do this.

 I don't want a new ~~daddy~~
father. I love my real Dad. I
smell his cologne, my "new dad",
and my arm rises again before I
can tell it to stop. I feel the
kitchen knife enter his chest,
but a jolt hits my arm, and the
point won't go in any more. Mark
wakes up and he's screaming and
looking down at his chest and
his eyes are SO big, and my
mo~~m~~ther wakes up too and she's
screaming too. I pull as hard as
I can on the handle, and the
knife comes up and blood starts
pouring from Mark's chest like
lava from a volcano. Before I
can back away the knife comes
down again, sliding right into
his chest, and it feels like
cutting a watermelon. I look up
to see my mother staring at me
with a look of terror, and Mark
has blood coming from his mouth

so I stab him again in the
stomach to stop the blood
because if the blood's coming
from lower down won't it not go
higher up?

My mother screams again and I
yell at her to shut the ~~*fuck*~~
hell up. I pull out the knife
and the smell of bad ~~*shit*~~ *feces*
hits me and I gag. My mother
tries to run but I point the
knife up in time to stab her in
the stomach too. The knife
points up and she falls down,
and I feel another stir as I
pull the knife out and her blood
comes out. I stop being scared
as I unzip—"

Wayne managed to pull himself from the morbid tale before reading any more. His hands, coated in sweat, smoothed the paper down on the desk's surface in front of him. It took all of his resolve to keep from screaming himself, as he pictured in his mind's eye Kristopher's every move, his cold, hard face, the blood-spattered kitchen knife clutched hard in his hand ...

Shaking his head once with a jerk to clear the memories not his own, he reached for the phone inches away from his right hand. Sliding his shaking finger across

54

the touch screen, he brought up the dial pad, pressing the three numbers he had only had to dial a few times before in his life.

"Nine-one-one, please state your emergency."

"Uh, yes, ma'am. Could you please connect me to the Jefferson Parish Sheriff's Office?"

"Is this a matter of urgency, sir?"

"Yes, ma'am. I may have a piece of evidence in a current murder investigation related to a student of mine. Can you patch me through, please?"

"Yes, sir. Please hold."

Sweat caused the phone to slip a bit in his grasp, necessitating a tightened grip as a new voice entered his ear. "JPSO, Officer Walls speaking."

"Yes, is Lieutenant, um, Parks, I think it was? Is she on duty?"

"Yes sir, hold on one moment, I'll put you through to her desk."

Muzak took place of the female officer's voice, smooth jazz fading in and out with the differing connections. Before he could begin to decipher the song, the husky voice of Lieutenant Parks broke through the noise. "This is Parks, can I help you?"

"Yes ma'am. I'm Wayne DePriest, we've spoken before."

"And that would have been about ...?"

"A student of mine, Kristopher Bates? You were trying to get his location."

The change in her voice was noticeable enough for Wayne to spot the difference. "Yes sir, of course. Actually, I have news on that front, if you'd like to hear it." A sad tone.

"Sure thing. Did you ever find him?"

"Yes sir, but unfortunately, we were too late to save him."

Wayne felt his blood run cold once more, felt his grip on the phone loosen in shock. "Wh-what do you...?"

"We found his body the next day. We thought he might have killed a local girl. Reports state she was his girlfriend, but it's unconfirmed. When we went back to his house, we found him behind the air conditioning unit in the back yard."

Wayne felt a burning sensation spread from his chest to his left shoulder, making him drop the phone in his right hand to the desk. He felt sick to his stomach, short of breath.

"Mister DePriest? Are you still there?"

-Fin.

~~*

C. Priest Brumley is a bipedal humanoid with an iron (ah, screw it: soft butter) will. His interest in writing came early, attempting to write his first book at the age of twelve. By the time he was in high shool, he had also developed a taste for graphic design, and continues to hone both skills to this day. A graduate of the Carville Job Corps Academy, he currently resides in New Orleans, LA, and can always be found online at his official Facebook page: **www.facebook.com/cpriestbrumley**

The Three Trials
Of
Atty Eve

Kris English

"Witch!"

"Burn in Hell!"

"Think of the children!"

Insults raged from all sides of the circle as the young woman huddled in rags in the centre of the mob. Women, holding children to their breasts, screamed and spat while men pounded pitchforks on the flagstones of the village centre.

"What on God's green earth is happening here?" a voice boomed across the baying crowd followed instantly by silence. Only the wind blowing through the trees and the soft whimper coming from the rags could be heard. Heads turned to observe the newcomer slowly edging a horse forward. Tall and imposing with a dark overcoat and a wide brimmed hat.

"Milord, we 'ave captured this witch," spoke a man, the village mayor.

"I received your message," the stranger replied, pushing his horse through the crowd.

Then, he spoke in a voice that carried across the square. "My name is Kristopher English, and I am the Witchfinder General."

"Very good, milord," the mayor said. "You must be here to oversee the trial."

"I do not see a trial, just a rabble of villagers baying for blood," the Witchfinder spat with contempt. "First, tell me about the witch and her crimes."

"Milord, her name is Atty Eve. She has lived in the village for eight years, we took her in as a child after we found her wandering in the woods," the mayor explained. "She has been filling the children's minds with stories, leading them away from salvation. Our Reverend has witnessed the children utter words in weird tongue and shake uncontrollably since talking to Mistress Eve."

"Mister Williams, lift the accused. I wish to see her."

61

A man stepped forward from behind the horse, pulling the woman to her feet; he brushed the long matted hair from her face. She stared defiantly at the Witchfinder.

"I must speak with the accusers first," he said. Two boys and an older girl stepped forward.

"What are your names?"

"If it pleases milord I am Ashley McKenna," the golden-haired teenager spoke first.

"I am Laurence Bastwick," a dark haired ten-year-old mumbled next looking towards the ground.

"My name is Robert Houghton," the shy eight year old finally replied.

"I wish for you to tell me your story," English commanded.

"Milord, Laurence, Robert and I all enjoy playing in the woods. Several weeks ago, we found Mistress Eve's home. She looked so pretty and her son sat upon the stoop singing like an angel." Ashley replied.

"Where is her son now?" the Witchfinder demanded.

"He is almost a man, and ran as soon as the village men came close to the home." The Mayor said.

"We shall capture him after we finish this trial," the Witchfinder replied. "Please, continue."

"Milord, we approached the house and were met by lovely smells of herbs. Mistress Eve began to tell us stories from *Malleus Maleficarum*, of dancing with the devil while denouncing the one true God. We began to dance and I felt funny, like she had put a spell on me. The boys took off their clothes, acting like wild animals," the teenager paused as the two younger boys looked sheepishly at the floor. "I danced unnaturally with the witch's son."

"How did you come to escape?" English asked.

"We woke up the next morning, in a clearing a little ways into the wood," Ashley replied staring at her feet.

"Lies!" Atty Eve spat. "Those little toads mocked my son and then this harlot tried to seduce him. He ignored her and she ran off."

"Shut your mouth, witch," Williams backhanded her.

"If all you have said is true, then she is truly a witch, but she must endure the Trials to prove her innocence."

Atty cried out in fear as Williams picked her up from the floor throwing her over his shoulder. The mob all followed to the fast flowing River Ouse.

"First is the trial by water, if she is innocent of all crimes, then she shall sink to the bottom and be met at the gates of Heaven by Jesus; if she is in league with the Devil, water spirits shall push her to the surface," Witchfinder English announced to the villagers.

Before the brackish water, stood a wooden platform with one end anchored to the ground and a long limb reaching over the water dangling a rope. Attached to the rope was a chair. Williams and the villagers bound Atty Eve's hands tightly as she watched them, subdued. Men from the village lifted her body, placing her on the chair, and letting it swing out across the water. The only sound was the creaking of the rope as the crowd fell into a hushed silence.

"Lower her down," the Witchfinder commanded.

The pair released the rope that was wound tightly lowering her into the water. Slowly, the water lapped up across the wooden chair, over the rags she was wearing, and into her lap, startling the young woman. She hissed with the coldness of the water as it went over her belly, chest, then finally lapped at her chin. Screaming wildly she tried to lift her head from the water, but it slipped over her mouth. She stared once more into the eyes of the villagers, then her head went under. The crowd let out a sigh as the seaweed like hair disappeared. Minutes passed and the Reverend stepped forward.

"She has gone to God now. He is opening his arms to welcome a new angel into his fold."

No sooner had he finished when the young woman emerged, very wet, but still alive.

"The Devil hath protected her," a woman cried.

Williams and the villager dragged her from the chair, as she coughed up black water, and hauled her in front of the Witchfinder.

"With God as our witness, we gave you a fair trial to prove you were innocent, but sometimes the Devil's hands can be strong," he intoned. "Now, we know Atty Eve is guilty. She must be hanged before the church."

A horse was brought forward and the witch was thrown over its back like a sack of potatoes as everyone moved towards the small stone church, which lay in the centre of the village. Some say the church was built when Jesus was born; others say the Romans built it. In the square beyond the church was a small fountain with a hastily erected structure to house the noose used for heretics and witches. Though this structure had seen no use, local militia had insisted upon it being built. Atty looked upon the structure with a degree of fear; two thick beams had been buried into the ground and a third lay atop them.

"Do you have anything to say before you are hanged, Mistress Eve?" the Witchfinder asked.

"I am innocent. That young lady tried to seduce my son, who in turn ignored her," Atty Eve said loudly over the other voices.

"Lies!" Ashley shouted.

"Witch!"

"You shall join the Devil in Hell," voices no longer separate, but as one, chanted at her.

"You have failed the trial by water, therefore, you shall be hanged. May God have mercy on your soul!"

Williams stepped forward carrying a noose, fitting it tightly around the neck of the bound woman. Atty choked briefly, then let out a deep breath as he picked her up throwing her over his shoulder. The villager placed a roughhewn ladder against the structure and Williams began to climb. Reaching the top, he took the other end of the rope and tied it securely around the beam. Without ceremony, he grabbed Atty and threw her away from him. The rope snapped taut, strangling the supposed witch. The crowd watched fascinated, seeing a hanging for the first time. She dangled, her legs jerking like a puppet on a string.

Some would say later, they heard the soft pluck of a bow or saw the arrow that caused it. Days later, the Witchfinder found the arrow, but by then rumours had already grown that the Devil had saved the Witch himself. The rope snapped causing her to crash to the ground gasping for breath, and for the second time, alive after a trial.

"The Devil is strong with this one," the Witchfinder said with glee, knowing this witch would be his crowning glory. "If she cannot be drowned and she cannot be hung, there is one way to kill a witch—by fire!"

Villagers were sent out to gather wood as darkness began to descend on the village. While the villagers worked installing a large stake into the ground, the Witchfinder watched impassively, his face shadowed by his hat.

"The Devil is at work tonight."

The Reverend stood next to the rider, indicating the moon, which was blood red.

"Indeed he is."

"Have you met many witches, milord?"

"Yes, they are dastardly and devious," the Witchfinder returned.

He went quiet as the last villager came forward and placed a bundle of sticks at the base of the stake. Atty Eve was bought forward and tied to the stake.

"Tonight is your hour of deliverance; confess your sins and God may yet help you in the afterlife."

65

"I have nothing to confess, my lord. I am innocent, but tonight innocent blood shall be spilt and I shall have my retribution in the next life. Ashley McKenna, Laurence Bastwick and Robert Houghton, your souls will be mine," she cackled with laughter.

The villagers screamed. Williams stepped forward and placed his torch to the wood. Instantly, crackling could be heard and *whoosh*, the wood began to flame snaking towards the sky.

The flames seemed to move slowly at first, but then they began to lick at Atty's feet. She began to scream from the pain and the heat. The flames got higher. Now capturing her rags and scorching her body. Not one of villagers would forget the screams, like the pained howls of a wolf or some unnatural creature. Time seemed to accelerate and the screams cut off as the woman died.

"My work here is done," the Witchfinder said and turned his horse away.

The Reverend blinked. He would later say it was a trick of the light, but he swore by the Lord Jesus, that he had seen the Witchfinder's eyes glow like the dying embers of red coal. The Reverend shuddered and the Witchfinder rode into the forest leaving the village behind. Some distance into the woods, he stopped and looked out.

"Do not worry child. I knew your mother," he said softly and the sixteen-year-old son of Atty Eve came into the light of the torch Williams held.

"You are the Witchfinder General," he said loudly.

"Hardly, but those simple villagers will believe anything."

"Who are you?" the boy asked.

"A friend of your mothers, she is now in my residence," the man said, taking off his hat. His face was made of pure shadow and where his eyes should be, were glowing red spots. He offered the boy his hand.

"Take my hand and join me."

"You are the Devil!"

*Kris English lives in the wilds of Norfolk, UK and has been writing since he was fifteen. Though currently unpublished he has a couple of books finished and is working on an internet serial. For musings by Kris English you can **visit http://archersscribe.wordpress.com/***

Welcome
to the
Afterlife

Jessica M. Kirkpatrick

Death, I knew him well. Too well, I realize now.

He's a portly fella, Death is, with thinning hair that is about the shade of straw. His hook nose was always in a romance novel of some sort. Last I saw, Nora Roberts was his latest obsession. That could've changed in the last few months... or was it years? I'm not really sure anymore. Time moves in circles now.

I was in the library when he walked in the door, ebony robes blowing around him. Seeing a scythe hanging from a belt holding a pair of blue jeans still startled me. The computers all blinked out at once as a small bellow eased through the stacks. The librarian looked up from the circ desk.

"Shhh!" She growled. Death stopped short.

"I'm sorry," he whispered. His face turned pink. Heat spread across my own cheeks. "Have you seen Kathy?"

"Computers."

Nodding, he walked over to the five or six computers against the wall. I turned more so he could see me better. He sat at a computer beside me.

"Hello."

"Hi," I responded. Facebook was holding most of my attention. Sally was getting married. "What'cha wants to see me for?"

"I have to talk to you, Kathy."

"'Bout what?"

"It's time," he said. I looked at him fully. Death leaned forward.

"Time for what?" I asked.

"I'm sorry, Kathy."

I stared into his blue eyes. They were like ice. A switch in my brain was flipped. "Oh."

He motioned for me to follow him. I logged out of Facebook and my email before returning the computer pass. Death led me to the reference section, the aisle too

73

slender for my post-baby body. He stopped me between two shelves.

"Reach for that dictionary," he ordered. I obeyed. I felt a hand on my back and that's the last I remembered.

According to AL protocol, I had to watch my death on an old movie reel.

"No one's died with DVDs and a DVD player, yet," the technician said, setting up the projection.

My hair looked terrible. Instead of being held in a gently pulled back ponytail, it was going everywhere. I hadn't bothered to brush it out. Death wasn't in the movie. According to the film I was going forward on my own accord. My black slacks were wrinkled and my blouse unbuttoned. Another fluke of the day. It was white. The tank underneath was stained, when we could see it. For once, there was something from my usual routine in my wardrobe choice. Every one of my tanks was stained with food. I stopped and turned. Looking up, I searched for the dictionary Death asked me to get down. It was on the very top shelf, wedged in tightly. Watching myself reach for a book, I gripped my pants leg.

Don't let me do that!

A camera change.

A grown man, shouting at the librarian for who knows what, shoved the bookcase as hard as he could. It started falling, hitting the one next to it. That one hit the next and soon there was a domino effect. I had to watch as the bookcases collapsed until they fell over poor old Kathy Jones.

There was a change of scene and I was crouching, covering my head. I hadn't gotten the dictionary all the way off the shelf. The case it was on had fallen against the one held up by the wall. There was a space for me to crouch. Not all the books had fallen off, yet. I was breathing hard in the video. And out of the video.

74

The grown man jumped on top of the first shelf, causing a butterfly effect. The vibrations caused the dictionary to fall off its metal shelf just as I moved my arms down. Someone had just asked me if I was okay. Poor chap.

"Yeah," I said. The dictionary—as thick as a brick and as big as a box—hit my head with a *crack!*

After the movie, I was taken to my room.

It was larger than my In Life room. A double bed took up the space by the wall furthest from the door. A white side table was beside it, with a lamp and alarm clock. They were all vintage. I had no closets, but a wardrobe sat to the left of the table, also white. My dresser from life sat to the right of the door, mirror hanging over it. A kitchenette, complete with fridge, was up against the left wall. It had a retro look, bright red. Ugly. I figured the fridge would be empty. I was wrong. Really, really, *really* wrong. It was stocked so full; almost everything fell out when I opened the door.

It took an hour to pick everything up. As I did, I noticed a lot of yogurt. Try three million of those little tubs you get from the super market. The stove was gas and I even had a microwave. Vintage, of course. A Victorian desk sat at the foot of the bed. No computer. No television. I didn't even have a stereo. Sighing, I nearly tripped over a short table. Black. Too short for chairs, I noticed the four brightly colored cushions arranged around it.

Death was sitting on the blue one.

"What on Earth is going on?" I asked, pacing. "I just saw my own death, but I can't be dead. My mother needs me not to mention my daughter who is *pregnant.* I'll never get to see my grandbaby. I'll never see my great-nephew. My ladies need me to change their diapers and make sure they eat. What about them?"

"Calm down, Kathy."

"I am not dead."

"Kathy, sit down. Have some food."

I did. Salmon sat in front of me. Various comfort and high fattening foods were with it on the plate. I didn't take a second bite. Death stared at the newspaper in his hands. He flipped it open. "New Comers" was the headline.

"Eat." It was a demand, not a request.

"I'm on a diet, Death." His eyes flew up to meet mine. They held no ice now, only sympathy.

"Calories don't count here."

I wasn't so sure I believed him. His hair now had the same shine that a crooked salesman had when he was about to sell you a lemon. It was slicked back. Even his suit, though attractive, looked sleazy. Lucky him, though. Not a single wrinkle. My outfit had been the one I had died in. I did notice that he had a Doctor Who tie.

"New or classic 'Who'?"

He smiled. The newspaper turned its page and a book appeared right before me. It floated in mid of the air. I grabbed it.

'Are You There, After Life? It's Me, Deceased', was its title. On the front cover was the picture of a corpse. It was macabre, yet comforting. Talk about a bizarre feeling. Death smiled like he knew what I was thinking. The salmon looked tasty.

"That book is meant to help you navigate this world."

"I can't be dead."

"Well, I am sorry."

I stared at him. Rouge, for some reason, adorned his cheeks. He wore eyeliner and...

Is that lipstick?

Death started strumming his fingers on the table. He seemed impatient.

"Are you the Other Mother?" I asked, jokingly. He only smiled whimsically.

"Ah, Neil Gaiman. Can't wait to reap him." His words made my blood run cold. I changed position on the cushion to relieve my back pa—"

76

"Wait! Why doesn't my back hurt?"

Death didn't say anything. Instead he looked at his—probably Swiss—watch like he was either bored or late for a date. Maybe he had to see Alice. It looked like he had a pocket watch, too. There was a bulge in his jacket.

I opened the book. The title page had a picture of Marilyn Monroe. She was posed quite conservatively, in a pair of long pants and a sailor blouse. The dark blue contrasted nicely with the white page. Her shoes were a pair of stilettos, red. I was sure she had never worn them ever in life. There was a red scarf over her head, and her eyes were covered by a nice pair of sunglasses. The only make up I could see was her bright red lipstick. Behind Marilyn was a beach.Turning the page, I saw the chapter titles.

'So now you're dead as a doorknob', was chapter one. Nice of them to be blunt. I scanned the chapter. It was mostly about how, now that I was dead, I was free of some of life's issues. No worries about meeting up with enemies, or buying food. When the fridge was empty, it would automatically fill again.

"This says that I don't have to worry about a thing."

"You don't. Kathy, this is how you spend time now. You make it your heaven or your hell," Death said. I leaned back to rest on my hands. The food begged me to eat it. I considered not obeying my stomach, but Death had said calories do not count. I began eating.

Between mouthfuls, I said, "This tastes really good."

Death smiled as he replied,

"Welcome to the After Life, Kathy Jones."

~~*

77

Jessica Kirkpatrick has been writing since fourth grade and is a Creative Writing major at Hollins University where she also minor in Sociology. Her mentor had been in her life since she was very young and she would have never picked up the fateful quill if she he never known her. July 2nd of 2013, she married the love of her life in that following October she had a son. Everything she writes is dedicated to her family.

Jessica writes horror and fantasy fiction. She's published the short story "Four Ghosts (After One Girl)" in Blood Moon Rising Magazine. Her first novel "Urban (Working Title)" is currently bei written. She hopes to release it sometime in 2015. In her spare time she crochets, reads, knits, participates in art, and sews.

You can follow Jessica at:

https://bwrthornportfolio.wordpress.com

http://jessicamkirkpatrick.tumblr.com

https://twitter.com/KirkpatrickJM

Absence Makes the Heart Grow Fonder

Rob Houglan

Beth woke with a start, blinking to clear her vision as the red numbers on her traitorous alarm clock sharpened enough to read.

"Shit!" she said as she scrambled out of bed and stumbled to the bathroom. A quick shower, a little makeup, and a hastily-arranged ensemble left her barely enough time to grab a few bites of leftover stir-fry. Grabbing her phone and purse, she dashed for the door, muttering "Be late, be late, just a little late." like a mantra as she half-ran, half-stumbled to the bus stop.

Seeing a few of the other regular passengers still standing there, she slowed enough to keep from looking crazed as she joined them to wait. Her breathing back to normal, she engaged in some meaningless chatter until the thunder of the bus' diesel signaled the start of another day at the rat race. As she boarded, she noticed a black sedan parked just down the street, sun glare off its windshield making it impossible to see inside. Trying to navigate the steps in her heels was enough distraction to keep her from thinking more about it. Finding her seat, she sighed as the bus lumbered away from the stop and crawled down the street.

The bus was crowded, and even early in the morning the air conditioner did its wheezing, clanking best to take the edge off of what was going to be a scorcher. Talking to Mrs. Lenore across the aisle, she was distracted by a man in the back who seemed to be staring at her. It was hard to tell since he was wearing black shades, but she had the sense that he was indeed watching her. Truth to tell, she was used to men looking at her, and she went back to her conversation.

Singly and in pairs, passengers got off at their stops, and when it was her turn, she stepped onto the sidewalk in front of Rushton Publishers. She went through the revolving doors, flashed her ID and a smile at the guard and crossed the lobby to the elevators, the button on the wall lighting in red when she pushed it. Looking around waiting

83

for the car to arrive, she saw the man from the bus standing at the security desk talking to the guard, who jerked a thumb in her direction. When the bell sounded, she ducked into the elevator and pushed the fifth-floor button until the door closed. She sighed again as the car gently rose.

On her floor, she exchanged some quick greetings and reached her desk, grumbling about the stack of files already waiting, leaning slightly in an unstable tower. Shifting it slightly, she took a minute to fix her hair and makeup then opened the first file and went to work. For once, the phone stayed silent long enough for her to make a dent in the stack before lunch. Her stomach growling, she returned to the elevator and rode the car back to the lobby. She was halfway across when the man from the bus approached her.

"Miss Tulliver," he said, not quite asking a question.

"That's me. Can I help you with something?"

"I need you to come with me, please."

"Where I'm going is to lunch and then back to work. Just tell me what you want so I can go."

"That will not be possible. Your presence is required elsewhere," he said, taking hold of her arm just above her elbow.

Living in a big city carries risks, abduction ranking high on the list, and so a young woman learns early to take care of herself. Unable to shake his grip on her arm, she ran her left foot down the inside of his right leg, stomping hard on his instep. As large as he was, a stiletto heel grinding into his foot made an impression, and, with a grunt, he let her go. As soon as she was free, she ran to the security desk to find it empty. Her luck running true to form, she went through the revolving door and turned left towards the Thai restaurant where she normally ate. She looked behind her but couldn't see the man who had accosted her in the milling, midday throng.

With a few elbows and a judicious shoulder, she made it to the restaurant and took a table in the back, facing the door. The place was packed, and she relaxed a little in her booth. No way anyone would try something in here.

She had just placed her order when she was joined at her table by another man, dressed the same as the first, down to the black sunglasses. She looked around for a waiter, a manager, someone to help her, but the man shook his head, a finger to his lips. Metal struck the underside of the table, and she risked a peek down to see the black barrel of a nasty-looking handgun aimed right between her thighs. Eyes wide, nostrils flared, she looked back at the man. Her voice cracked when she spoke.

"What do you want from me? Are you a cop? What have I done?"

"You have broken your word, and we are here to rectify that oversight."

"What word? What are you talking about? I haven't promised you anything!"

"Incorrect, Miss Tulliver. You have indeed made a promise, and we are here today to collect."

"Bullshit! You people need to leave me alone, or I'm calling the cops!"

"That would be inadvisable, not to mention useless. You will come with me, now. Your only choice is in whether or not I must carry you."

Another desperate look around found no one close enough to help her. She considered screaming, but that cannon under the table was a strong deterrent. On shaky legs, she rose from the table and, firmly in his grasp, she went outside. Waiting at the curb was the black car she had seen at the bus stop. The rear door opened, and she was pushed inside. She skidded along black leather as she felt cotton against her nose and mouth. A startled gasp, then it all went dark.

She awoke naked, strapped down to a bed in a stark white room. A bright, unshielded ceiling light forced her eyes into tearing slits. Razors slid along her throat as she

85

coughed to clear it, and, finally regaining her voice, she screamed and sobbed against the pain. She thrashed against her restraints hard enough to risk toppling the bed, all to no avail. No one came; no one answered. The strap against her chest bit cruelly with every panicked breath she took. Her mind thudded to the drumbeat of "why, why, why, why" as she fought her fear, fought her doubts, fought her despair. Her thoughts whirled in useless eddies, impossible plans swirling frantically in her desperation. She sobbed anguished prayers to a God she had abandoned years ago, bleated frenetic promises to live a better life in return for her salvation. After what seemed like hours, she languished, spent, lying in her sweat and tears, shivering as goose bumps rose on her flesh.

Finally, a man and woman came to her bed and rolled it out of the room, ignoring her questions and curses. Down a hallway, around a corner, down another hallway, until finally they stopped in a large room full of machinery and equipment. Several figures were standing around a metal table, wearing blue surgical scrubs and white masks. She felt the prick of a needle as her restraints were removed and she was transferred to the frigid metal table, a powerful spotlight shining brightly enough to make her close her eyes. She struggled feebly as her thoughts spun free, to final surrender, to drift on a cloud as she relaxed against her will. A woman bent over her and lowered her mask.

"Miss Tulliver, we want to thank you for your compassion and dedication to helping others. Because of the sacrifice you make here today, another life will go on to achieve its full potential. You will be remembered and honored for what you do here today. Thank you so very much."

Her tongue having a mind of its own, she asked, "What conpashun? What are you talking 'bout?"

"Why, dear, I am talking about this," she said, holding up Beth's driver's license, the backside showing. "You signed the organ donor clause, and because of you, a

86

young man in desperate need of a heart is going to be returned to full health and vigor. Because you and those like you make the ultimate sacrifice, the world is a better place. Thank you, thank you, once again, thank you."

"But I'm still 'live."

"But of course, dear! What good would your heart be if we waited until you were dead? That young man needs it now, and because of you, he will have it."

She was sinking further into darkness with every passing second. She found the strength and curiosity for one last, "Who are you?"

The last thing she heard before that final dark passing was, "I thought you knew. I am his mother."

Rob Houglan, Akron Ohio, author of "Hump Day".
A writer even as a young child, he has been writing
horror, fantasy and science-fiction stories all of his life to
give expression to the voices in his head. Not satisfied with
the "real" world, he spends his time creating new ones,
inhabited with interesting people doing unusual things
that don't always conform to the laws of physics.

Kill ROb.

Josette Weiss

Larry woke and sat straight up in his sweat drenched bed. He wiped his face and said, "Da' fuck going on?"

It was another one of those crazy dreams. He shook his head and climbed out of bed. Maybe he just needed to get some ice water and chill for a little bit? Yeah. He glanced at the clock. Just like every morning for the past week, the clock read three on the dot.

Jebus. He walked into the kitchen, grabbed some ice water, and wandered into the computer room. He sat at the desk a moment, unsure if he really should turn the machine on. In his head, he wanted to write the next chapter of his WIP, but he knew he wouldn't. He reached forward, clicked the button and found Facebook.

"The bastid," Larry swore under his breath.

He checked the usual places first—the debate group with the crazy religion spouting fucks and then with one of his favorite groups, 'The Unblocked Writers'. Of course, there were some drive-by writers spamming their books on the wrong day. One claimed his book was a 'masterpiece'. Another claimed they had an instant best seller, guaranteed. Lazy good for nothing fucks.

Larry deleted and banned these wannabes and never-wills. Seconds before he left the group, another comment popped up. It wasn't a spammer. No this was a weird comment, from a new member by the name, Sammael Mammon. Larry scratched his chin. He'd seen that name before, but where? Maybe the new guy was part of a batch of members he'd recently approved, and that's where he remembered him from. He shrugged and sipped the ice water.

The comment read: "He wants you to do it."

Larry almost asked, "Do what?", but something deep inside told him not to post. Something was off. Whatever. Larry yawned, walked back into the dark bedroom and climbed into bed. Seconds later he was snoring.

The alarm went off at six in the morning. Larry grappled with the clock and finally threw the damned thing on the floor. Jebus. He had to wake up and go to work. Damn job took up all of his time.

Larry eased out of bed, showered, dressed, and sat in front of the computer again. He had thirty minutes before he had to be at the job. He sighed. What he needed to do was write a couple of paragraphs on his unfinished novel *Obey*, but instead he logged onto Facebook.

More fucking spam on the wrong day. He deleted and banned the stupid fucks and looked for the post from Sammael Mammon. He couldn't find it. Maybe Sammy boy deleted it after discovering he put it in the wrong group. It could happen, right?

Larry moved the mouse to exit the group and another post from Sammy popped up. Da' fuck?

This post stated: "You forgot the coffee."

Larry clicked out of the group and glanced at the clock. He did forget his morning cuppa' coffee. This didn't make any sense at all. Okay, he'd just swing by Starbucks and grab a 'Vente' something and enjoy the workday. Yeah.

During a break, Larry checked Facebook on his smartphone. The other admins must have taken care of any spam, for he didn't notice any, but really he was looking for a post from Sammy boy. Nothing.

Then he noticed Rob had posted a comment. Larry rolled his eyes. The over-talkative fuck wrote five paragraphs and didn't even get to the point. Typical. He decided to have a little fun with Rob and posted a wisecrack comment. Rob instantly replied with another six paragraphs about nothing. Jebus! How does Rob post so much gibberish so fast?

A post from Sammy boy appeared on Rob's thread. It read: "He forgot the coffee too and his cigarettes."

Larry sat back and waited to see what Rob would say to Sammy, but Rob just continued spewing a lot of something about nothing. It was as if he couldn't see

Sammy's posts. After a moment, Larry checked with the other admins. No, none of them okayed a Sammael Mammon and none of them could see any posts by the guy.

Da' fuck?

Lunch time. Larry sat outside, hoping the chilly air in Philadelphia would help him figure out what da fuck was going on in Unblocked Writers. Who was this Sammael Mammon guy?

He checked his phone. More of the never-ending bullshit from Rob, but the last comment made the little hairs on Larry's neck stand up.

The comment was from Sammy of course. It read: "He lives in Ohio. You have vacation time coming."

DA' FUCK?

Then his cell phone rang. Larry yelled, "Shit!" and jumped off the bench. This shit was crazy. First, the nightmares and then this crap? He rubbed his temples. The phone rang again. He glanced at the screen. Why da' fuck was his boss calling him? He glanced at the time. He still had ten minutes of lunch, but what the hell?

"Yes sir?"

The boss said, "Larry, we're selling out. Take your vacation as soon as possible or you'll lose it. I'll do my best to keep everyone employed, but I won't have much say over anything in two weeks' time."

Larry muttered under his breath, but said, "What? I don't understand."

The boss said, "I know, this came out of left field for me too. Just take your vacation and cross your fingers that we'll all have jobs when you get back."

The boss hung up and Larry let loose a string of profanity. He did not need this shit right now! Christmas was in four weeks. His nephews and nieces were expecting gifts from him.

His phone beeped. He had a notification. He walked back toward the office, still pissed, and scrolled down to see what the phone wanted. Facebook said someone had commented on a post he was following. He swore again. He wasn't following any posts, but Facebook must know something he didn't. He checked the notification. Sammy posted again. This time, the comment read: "The flight leaves in six hours. Your ticket is on the counter."

Larry turned off the phone and said, "Screw you, ya' fucktard."

The rest of the day passed by quickly. Right before he was about to log out for the day, he received an email saying that his vacation was approved. Larry scratched his head. He didn't request any vacation time. Maybe the boss did it for him? Whatever, he rushed home, thinking he would have a few drinks and watch Romo lead the Cowboys to another victory.

After entering his house, he noticed an envelope on the counter. He opened it, revealing a one way ticket to Ohio. The flight left in two hours.

"Da' fuck? I didn't purchase any tickets."

His phone beeped. He glanced down and saw ten posts, all from Rob, each at least seven paragraphs long. Damn it! He had enough of this 'bullshyte'. He rushed to the bedroom and threw a handful of clothes into an overnight bag. It was time for Rob to go down.

Philadelphia was cold. Ohio was fucking freezing! He took a cab to Rob's neighborhood and paid the man. The cab zipped away, leaving Larry standing in a snowstorm. Thankfully it just started. It was the middle of the night, so no one saw him as he stood quietly, staring at the nice house with one lone light blazing in the darkness.

His phone beeped. He glanced down. That was odd. He forgot his charger and the phone was dead, and yet he still received messages from Sammael Mammon.

The message read: "The wife and kid are gone for a few days. Wifey's mom had a bad case of acid reflux, nothing to be concerned with of course, but she wanted to spend some time with her parents. Rob didn't go. Ya know, he has all of that lawyer type stuff he pretends to do. :)"

"Da' fuck? A smiley face?"

Larry shoved his phone back in his pocket and shook the large wet snowflakes off of his head. He walked into Rob's yard. The rest of the neighborhood was dark and silent. Larry glanced around. It was a nice house, two stories, picket fence, and toys scattered on the front lawn.

What was he doing there?

The phone beeped. It was Sammael, yet again. The message read: "He's awake and on the second floor. The door to the garage is unlocked. He forgot to check. Sigh, even after wifey reminded him."

Larry walked to the garage door. He hesitated, then placed his hand on the ice-cold knob. It turned and Larry stepped inside the warm house. He exhaled and relaxed. This was easier than he thought it would be.

He tip toed through the house, stepped over scattered toys, stopped at the stairs and listened. He heard the clickety clack of the keyboard. The man must stay up at all hours typing 'shyte'. Larry eased up the stairs. Did Rob have a dog? Larry racked his brain to remember if he'd ever commented about being a dog owner. Damn, the bastid wrote so much, and Larry never really read it all. Whatever, Sammael and Facebook didn't say anything about a dog. He would assume there wasn't one.

He paused at the doorway of what had to be Rob's study. Large books were scattered, opened, all over the floor, much like the toys outside. Crumbled up paper was discarded into an over flowing trashcan. The room smelled like cigarettes and fresh coffee.

Larry heard Sammy's voice in his head. Sammy whispered, "Wait for it ..."

Rob leaned down to pick up a discarded cigarette and Larry rushed in, grabbed the keyboard and wrapped the wire around Rob's neck.

97

Rob gurgled something and Larry eased up on the taut wire. He said, "What?"

Rob said, "Obligations to guillotine must be requested beforehand and then dispersed within the society to be discussed and recommended or not. The ..."

Larry screamed and said, "You don't make any sense! You just use big words to bullshit your way through life!"

Larry dragged Rob over to the window. Thankfully instead of struggling or fighting back, Rob simply yammered away. Larry didn't pay any attention to the crap Rob said.

The cord was not long enough to reach. Damn it! He used one hand to push the slightly open window all the way up. Rob must have had it cracked to let out the cigarette smoke. Larry yanked the cord and the entire computer, monitor and all moved. Larry laughed and pushed Rob, still talking non-stop, out of the window.

He jumped to the side as the computer crashed to the floor, caught with the plug in the wall, and then the cord gave. Fuck! Larry glanced outside and watched as Rob landed in an awkward position outside on the frozen lawn. Damn! Rob continued to talk.

Larry raced back to the garage. He needed to stop Rob before he called for help. Once in the garage, Larry noticed a straight edged shovel leaning against the wall.

Sammy's voice laughed with glee and said, "Now there's a weapon."

Larry grabbed the shovel and ran around to the back yard where Rob landed. Thankfully Rob was still there, hunched over in a ball and cradling his broken arm.

Rob said, "My humerus fractured as I collided with the terra firma, resulting in copious amounts of physical and mental suffering."

Larry raised the shovel and said, "Shut da fuck up already!"

He jammed the shovel down, on Rob's neck. Rob's head lolled to the side. Blood spurted out of the headless corpse. Larry gasped for breath and leaned against the shovel a moment.

Rob's head said, "A beheading was imminent and unforeseen. Sorrowful and yet poignant with an uncharacteristic..."

Larry slammed the shovel down over and over, until there was nothing left but pieces and parts. He screamed "Shut up! Shut up! Oh my fucking God, shut the hell up!"

Finally, exhausted, Larry limped back to the garage, dragging the bloodied shovel behind him. Even beheaded and dismembered, Rob had continued to jabber. Larry wiped the sweat from his forehead and placed the shovel back where he found it. He had noticed something useful inside. This should shut the fucker up for good. Larry cackled as he trudged back to where Rob's body laid scattered in the backyard. He could still hear Rob's voice.

Sammael's voice broke in, "Damn, can't I get a word in edge wise here? Jebus, I hope he shuts up when he arrives in hell. Gawd, please sew his mouth shut."

Larry squirted fire starter on the dismembered body and tossed pieces of cardboard around. He flicked the lighter and touched it to the cardboard, then squirted the house as the fire caught and jumped at the flammable liquid.

He backed away as the house blazed. He laughed and sat on the wet ground. His phone beeped. He glanced at the dead phone and a post from Sammael Mammon appeared: "Time for coffee."

Larry stood and said, "Yeah, coffee sounds good right now."

~~*

Josette Weiss lives in Tennessee with her husband. She has always wanted to be a writer, even as a toddler she would flip through picture books and speak gibberish, making up her own story on each page. In 2013 Josette's dreams came true. She published her first book, Haunted Reality, which is about an evil house haunted by more than just ghosts. Before the year was out, she published four more books. You can find more information on Josette Weiss at her website: **www.Crossbonespublications.webs.net**

volta

Vicki Barnes

The *clunk, clink* ricochet as the iron bars slammed together echoed through the empty halls, the violent intro to the night's usual lullaby. A somber tune played well by uniformed guards. Minions to God and man's authority, our keepers as governed by the law of humans.

Someone sang,
Someone cried,
Someone silent,
Someone died.
Does it matter?
No not at all.
Death row.
My home.
My final call.

I turned the pages of my book, reading the words of someone long since dead. A forefather of my kind. Volta, the title read at the top of the page, the final dance of my soul. I had read this incantation like reciting a prayer, it was memorised, but it gave comfort to see the words. To read it one more time.

My final hours ticked by. The sound of the clock was quiet that night. I listened to the scurry of the vermin, the scratching of their claws on the cold stone floors. Somewhere close a pipe dripped. Someone used the lavatory. Someone passed gas. Such primitive creatures, they did not know what was coming for them. My neighbours. I was thankful this was my final night.

"Volta," I said the word, said it slowly. It resonated in my head with its calming wings, soothing my mind. No, I was not afraid of my final journey. I did not fear the death I faced the next day.

We all make sacrifices.

For her, my love. I did it for her. They could take my body, my empty shell. They could lay it bare and carve it open, but they would not take me. Not my soul, not what was mine, my spirit. I was meant to be here. This was not their choice to take me.

105

Oh, I had to be punished, that was certain. I understood it. I deserved that much. A failure to my master, I understood his lessons. These were his teachings, but he had given me a way. A way to redeem myself and show him that I served him as I was meant.

Lucifer. My father. My keeper.

I was nothing more than a retarded vessel that served him with my own greed. It was a mistake and did not go unpunished.

An insult.

I was weak. I understood that as I lay on my cot in my cell. I could not help myself. She was a tease, those eyes, the way they spoke. Her mouth, the way it moved. So inviting. Calling to me and I could not help myself. I was a victim to the lure of a woman, like many men before me.

She was not mine to have. Her breasts, small and soft. Like a defiant child I took what was not mine and spoiled it. I was a fool. I knew that. I did not deserve the second chance that I had been given, but I was thankful.

Another chance to find Lucifer his Catherine, she wasn't mine. I had read it in my book, it was all there. Find the girl, Catherine, ensure she is pure, offer her to him and he would come. He would claim his Catherine and in return, power. So much power. All I had to do was leave her pure, her innocence was his to sacrifice, but I was weak. He used the humans to punish me.

She hadn't been pure though. It was a lie, shown in the eyes of the boy who interrupted me as I defiled her. Eyes the same as hers. The same mouth. Her child. She was a whore and not worthy, that was why she had to die. That was why I took her life. It was not my fault that the followers of God did not understand.

I closed my eyes on my last night. I pictured her face, sweet and unmoving. Dead. Sent back to whence she came, so she may be reborn to fix the crimes she had committed. It was not for her to give herself to other men. She was not supposed to do that.

When the guards claimed me from my cell to take me on that walk, the one that all the inmates feared, delicious excitement swirled within my chest.

"Volta." One word, but it would be my release from this body and into the next. The judge vowed I would never walk this earth again, but he was wrong.

A guard's thick hand grabbed my arm. "Silence," he said. His voice lacked any form of command that I would recognise and obey.

Soon, though. Soon his time would come. We would meet again. Not here, not in this place, but within his lifetime. He would remember me. He would never forget me.

They laid me down on the steel table and I saw her through the glass. Not Catherine. No, she was dead and gone. But a face so similar, so delicate. The weeping sister, come to bear witness to my execution.

The straps went on, the needles pierced my skin, but they would not keep me there. This was not what I was meant for. I did not wince nor cry. I did not fight them. I watched.

The innocent boy by his aunt's side. He stared at me. Eyes that knew me. I stared back. His soul was tainted, he had seen. He had been there when his mother had died. It had been unfortunate. I did not see the need to take him too. He was nothing to me, until then. My new vessel. Perfect, just for me.

"Any last words?" They asked.

Yes, yes. "Volta, volta."

There was a frown on my executioners face. I did not care and neither did he. It wouldn't matter. None of it would matter.

I stared at the boy. Watched his soul through his eyes as the hot liquid began to fill my veins.

"Volta," I said.

The leaping dance.

The soul dance.

The boy and I, we danced. From our bodies. Unseen to those in the room. "Volta," the incantation repeated like a mantra.

My destiny. My choice. I was chosen to find her. Catherine.

I opened my eyes. New eyes. Innocent eyes that had seen death.

My rebirth. I watched my old shell through the glass slip from this world. A gift to the boy. His horror welcomed death. I did not. He could have it, it was his to keep.

It was a fair trade. It ended the suffering of his tormented soul.

I grinned and clutched the hand of my new aunt.

"Volta," I said as I breathed in the air of my freedom.

~~*

Vicki Barnes is crazy... Not that bio. Vicki Barnes is a writer, she has been writing since forever. First published when she was five in the local newspaper, she still writes today. For a long time she spent her time writing as a gamer, writing on online saga for one of the gaming sites (since gone, sadly) Now Vicki is working on her novel somewhere between studying for her degree in psychology. A lover of the fictional world, Vicki resides in the North of England and can usually be found online on facebook when not writing or gaming.

www.facebook.com/AuthorVictoriaBarnes

What Would Brando DO?

Wayne DePriest

In the blackest of leather, he walked into the bar. A Wild One. A modern day Brando. At least that's the way Oliver Prender thought of himself; that's what he wanted to be. The reality was a bit different. Oh, he had the leather jacket. He had the oiled, slicked back hair, even if it was prematurely thinning. He had the swagger. He had the bill of the Johnny cap tugged down slightly to the right. It might have been the pallor that took away some of the effect. It might have been his hundred forty-seven pounds draped over the six foot two inch frame. All in all, he didn't garner the sort of attention he thought he should from the dozen or so people scattered around the bar. What he did get were nods in his direction accompanied by half smiles that might have indicated humor or disbelief. One or two patrons tapped the shoulders of others and indicated Oliver with a 'Get this' thrust of a thumb.

"Beer?" Oliver said, as he got to the bar. He tried for a baritone command. He got a tenor half question.

"Can you narrow it down for me, buddy?" The bartender was a gray haired beefy guy, with forearms the like of which Oliver believed his own would be if he kept at the weights.

"Um ..." Oliver tried to think of a brand of beer. A commercial popped into his head. "Miller."

The bartender raised one eyebrow in question, a trick Oliver thought was pretty cool and had tried to master as he stood in front of the mirror every morning, wishing he had more beard to shave so he wouldn't have to shave.

"Lite," Oliver added in response. "Miller Lite."

A guy in a brown leather coat three stools away grinned. Oliver could see the grin in the mirror behind the bar. It wasn't pretty. Neither the grin nor the mirror. The mirror was grimy with smoke and fingerprints and God knows what else. The grin was cruel and missing three teeth on the left. *Well, technically the missing teeth were on the right because of the reverse effects of looking in the mirror.* The visual adjustment rationale came unbidden into Oliver's head. Weird stuff like that had a way of doing that. He wondered if he should do something about the guy who grinned.

WWBD? What Would Brando Do?

Something cool for sure. Something so cool and, at the same time, so badass that every other tough guy in the joint would know that Marlon Brando was nobody to fuck with. Something like a casual backhand to the grinning mouth; a backhand that would leave the guy spitting blood and several more teeth. *With whom nobody should fuck.* That was the problem right there. Brando would be dropping this guy like a bad habit. Brando would be beating the guy like a rented mule. All Oliver Prender could do was correct his own grammar.

"Two seventy-five," the bartender said as he set a bottle on the bar.

Oliver pulled the leather wallet from his back pocket with a practiced ease, thanks to the hours in front of the full length mirror on the back of his bedroom door. But he fumbled with the stiff new leather and the tight snaps. When they finally gave, he dropped the wallet. It hit the edge of the bar and fell, stopped six inches above the floor, and swayed back and forth on the silver chain looped to his broad leather belt.

Oliver blushed and hauled the wallet back up to his hand. *Thank God I zipped the zippers.* He flipped the flap back, tugged open one of the zippered pockets and, shielding the contents from the bartender and the guy in the brown coat and bad teeth, carefully separated three dollar bills from the sheaf of nineteen and laid them on the bar. "Keep it," he said.

The bartender looked at Oliver, looked at the three dollar bills and picked them up. "Thanks. Thought for a minute you might be a tightwad. Now I can get that operation."

"Operation?" Oliver asked with concern.

"Yeah. On my eyes."

Oliver squinted, wishing he'd worn his glasses. But cool guys don't wear glasses and his eyes were too sensitive for contacts. *Besides, it's only a little farsightedness.* If he squinted he could see just fine. So he squinted. "They look fine to me."

"Yeah. They look okay. But I see dumb asses."

The guy in the brown coat was looking at Oliver, grinning. "What the hell are you supposed to be?"

Oliver ignored him, concentrating on another sip of beer. He rotated the bottle in the wet ring on the bar, the way he'd seen actors do it in movies. They always looked so pensive when they did it. He put on his best pensive look; thoughtful, perusing the mysteries of the universe or perhaps the ways of a woman. It made him look slightly daft.

"Hey!"

A finger poked him in the left shoulder, knocked him just a little off balance.

"I said 'What the hell are you supposed to be?' Don't you hear so good?"

It was the guy in the brown coat that Oliver could now see was dirty; the leather cracked in several places. He was standing next to Oliver, one hand behind his back, the other with a finger extended for another poke.

WWBD?

Now, this is where Brando would calmly say something like, *'I hear real good. I hear the ambulance coming to take you in for repairs.'* Then Brando would slip off the stool while the guy was busy on that, and Brando would clip him on the jaw, quickly, efficiently, and the guy would drop to the floor. Brando would finish his beer so cool and calm and not even look at the guy he decked until he was ready to leave. Then he might kick the guy in the nads. That was Brando. But he was Oliver, so he thought about the guy's coat and was willing to bet, and give three-to-one odds, that the guy didn't have a painting of a leather-clad pig astride a Harley with 'Hog Wild' in dripping, blood-red letters below it on the back of *his* jacket.

So it wasn't any Brando bravado that came out of Oliver's mouth. It was just an answer to the guy's question. "I hear just fine. I was just thinking."

The guy grinned, exposing the gap in his teeth. "That's funny. So was I. Know what I was thinking?"

"How could I? I'm not telepathic."

"I was thinking if you could guess what's behind my back?

"I don't know."

"Guess. That's how this works, buddy. I got something behind my back. You get to guess what it is."

"If something is behind you, technically it's in front of your back. So behind your back is really in front of you. And I can see that you don't have anything in the hand in front of you."

"The fuck is that supposed to mean?"

"Ed." the bartender cautioned.

"What?"

"Let it rest."

"What?" Ed repeated. "I asked the guy a simple question. I can't ask a question now?"

"Let the guy finish his beer." To Oliver: "Drink up, fella. Maybe find another bar."

But Oliver didn't want to find another bar. What Oliver really wanted was for the guy in the brown coat to go away. What Oliver really wanted was for this sudden feeling of unease to be a reaction to the beer and not the presence of the other man. What Oliver really wanted wasn't going to happen and, somehow, he knew it. In a lifetime of being singled out for attention, he learned to recognize the signs. He took another drink from the bottle, chugged a couple of swallows. The third chug didn't get swallowed because

Oliver's epiglottis decided it was a good time to flip over for a breath of fresh air. His lungs then protested the invasion of beer and made a concerted effort to expel the invader with enough force to send the beer back up Oliver's throat. His mouth filled. Then over filled. The excess rushed through his sinus cavities and out his nose about the same time the bubble of expelled air caused enough pressure to force his mouth open.

Things might have been all right if Oliver had been facing the bar when the little flap of tissue in his throat betrayed him. But Ed had just poked Oliver again and Oliver had just turned his head toward the guy. So the beer and the snot and whatever else might have been clinging to several mucus membranes in Oliver's head landed mostly on the side of the Ed's face and splashed down onto the left shoulder of the dirty brown coat.

Oliver's head was bent down, so he didn't see the big overhand right. The detonation of pain as his right cheekbone shattered caused his vision to strobe. As he tumbled off the stool, Oliver saw the guy in the brown coat flicker in and out of sight. He felt something pop in his right shoulder when he hit the floor. Another blast of pain wrapped loving arms around him and squeezed real tight, tight enough to make him scream and fart in an off-key duet. Flat on his back, he tried not to move; tried real hard, but it hurt so bad. His face and then his shoulder and then his face again and the guy in the brown coat was leaning over Oliver and the guy wasn't laughing or even smiling, but he had his fist clenched and his arm cocked and he looked meaner than Chino in 'The Wild One'.

WWBD?

Right then Oliver Prender didn't give two farts in a windstorm what Marlon Brando would do. What he cared about was not getting hit again because he was pretty sure he couldn't handle any more pain without pissing in his jeans. The bartender must have known because he leaned over the bar and grabbed the brown leather coat and jacked the guy back against the bar hard enough to make him grunt.

"Goddammit, Ed!"

"What'd you expect me to do? The little prick threw up on me."

"You should've left him alone like I told you. Now we gotta call an ambulance. Cops and shit are gonna be crawling all over and there goes my business for the night."

"No." The bartender and the brown coat turned at the sound of Oliver's squeak. He was up on his left elbow, waiting for the a little ebb in the tide of agony. "No ammunce. No cos. I'n okay." His mouth wasn't working right. It hurt when he moved his jaw. It hurt when he didn't.

"You're fucked up, kid," the bartender groused. "Your face is all crooked. You need a doctor."

Oliver struggled to his knees, used a stool to lever himself to his feet. The bartender was blurry. Ed, he of the dirty brown coat, wasn't any more distinct. Oliver shook his head. Bad idea. Really bad idea. The pain was one thing. Hearing the broken bones in his face grate against one another was a whole different level of experience.

WWBD?

Brando would come storming off the floor, hurt or not. Brando would be on the guy in the brown coat like stink on shit. Brando would deal so much pain on the bastard that his own injuries would be a hangnail in comparison. All Oliver could manage was a stumble against the stool as he fumbled with the zipper on one of the jacket pockets. "No cos,' he repeated and winced at the pain, then groaned at the agony of the wince.

"Jesus, Ed, get him up on the stool."

"Fuck him."

"Goddammit, help him onto a stool."

Ed stepped forward, put his hands in Oliver's armpits and lifted, smiling as he worked his fingers into the damaged shoulder joint. The injured man screamed as the cartilage in his separated shoulder tore. He pulled his left hand out of the jacket pocket and Ed's eyes widened at the click of the switchblade opening. His eyes widened even more when Oliver, with twenty-six years of frustration behind the effort, slid the blade into the softness under the brown coat and jerked his arm sideways. Ed dropped Oliver and fell backwards, hands clutching at his gaping stomach.

Oliver bounced off the stool and crashed to the floor face first. The broken cheekbone shattered even more. The orbital socket of his left eye, denied the support of the heavier cheekbone, collapsed. His left eye popped out of the socket and dangled by the optic nerve. Three small pieces of splintered bone punctured Oliver's frontal lobe, severing the medial artery.

In his last moment of consciousness, he thought:

WWBD?

Somewhere, in all the pain, Oliver Prender decided even Brando had his limits.

A tall, mustached and rarely serious man, Wayne lives and writes in a suburb of Minneapolis with two cats, one wife and the normal compliment of spiders. On any given day Wayne can be found flying in the face of convention. After convention brushes him away, Wayne flies in the face of adversity. When he isn't flitting around annoying time-honored concepts, he writes a poem or a hundred or shoots pool or kills someone in a book....like his newest release "The Button Man."

You can follow Wayne at:

https://www.facebook.com/wdwriter

http://www.lulu.com/spotlight/awriter

http://www.amazon.com/Wayne-DePriest/e/B004XFVW8M/ref=sr_tc_2_0?qid=13 89020306&sr=1-2-ent

Meat the parents

the

Moira Briggs

In this world, this world I'm stuck in, I learned that people who do bad things deserve to be punished. If you hurt someone, you get hurt back times three. And I am willing to enforce that on people who deserve it.

"Hello sweetie" my mother said, walking into my room.

"I told you to knock," I said.

"This is *my* house," my mother replied coldly. "I can knock or not knock on the door when I want to."

I looked up at her "Do you think you can control me?" A faint growl escaped my lips.

My mother walked over and put her nose to mine "Yes. I. Am. Your. Mother."

She punctuated Mother with a bit of spit shooting at my face before strolling out of my room, slamming the door behind her. My mother. Her friends addressed her as Lisa. Oh Lisa, what a nice woman you were. Kind, sweet, beautiful. But you had no idea what your daughter was thinking. You had no idea, but you would. Soon ...

I walked into the kitchen nonchalantly, as happy as a clam and oh what a sick joy was building within me. My mother was talking on the phone and I knew who with. My therapist would have conversations with her for hours, suggesting medications and treatments that my mother would set aside, decline. I grabbed an apple and sat down at the table next to her. The kitchen was small but not too small. A white linoleum floor, a black fridge, breakfast bar and plenty of cabinets to spare. A small circular wooden table sat in the middle with three wooden chairs.

"Mom—" I was saying when I was cut off by a sharp "Shut up. I'm on the phone."

I stood and threw away my untouched apple. When the garbage can closed, it made a soft clunk.

"Shut-up!" she said. "Now leave or stay here and shut your mouth!"

As I sat down, I felt a rage building inside me.

"I'm sorry," my mother said into the phone, "I'll call you in a few days if I'm free. My daughter is misbehaving. Yes. Yes goodbye."

The chair scraped against the ground making a soft squeak. My mother screamed "SHUT UP!"

I lost it.

Screaming, I ran over to my mother and smashed her in the head with my fist. I heard a slight crack as my knuckles smashed her crown and she let out a yowl. I took duct tape out of one of the cabinets and tore off a double arm length strip of tape. I forced my dearest Lisa's arms against her chair and wrapped the tape around her like a mummy, I used an extra piece to cover her mouth.

Where should I do what I will with her?

One place came to me: the garage. I grabbed the back of the chair and dragged it along the hallway.

I stopped halfway to run into my room and grab a pair of old gloves. I needed to make sure no prints were left. Thanks for letting me watch all those murder mystery shows mom.

I walked back to where I left her and continued down the hallway, until we reached the stairs.

Thump! Thump! Thump!

I dragged her down the stairs to the middle of the garage and ripped the strip of tape from her mouth. She screamed. I smiled. A beautiful moment in my life.

"WHATTHEHELLDOYOUTHINKYOU'REDOINGLETMEG OYOU'REGONNABEINBIGTROUBLE!!"

Wearing a smile, I picked up a wrench from the floor, walked over and raised my arm.

"Shut up." I swung my arm down, bringing the metal tool across Lisa's face.

Her lips broke, no, tore open with a fountain of blood. She began to cry, tears streaming down her face. I grabbed a screwdriver and with a growl, drove it into the middle of her forehead. Contentment filled me. Blood ...

everywhere. A loud shriek bled into a groan then became silence. I had a slight smile on my face as I carried my mother into a closet in the garage and locked the door. Nobody came to check on me and the police never came.

* * *

It happened again.
On Halloween.
My father got me really pissed.
"You cannot stay up!" he yelled.
Josh is his name.
"I'm gonna stay up no matter what!"
"YOUR GONNA GET IN BED AND STAY IN THERE OR ELSE I'LL PUT YOU TO BED MYSELF!!"
A faint growl escaped my lips as he closed the door, then a smile spread across my face. Oh Josh, you made the same mistake as Lisa did, you sorry, sorry, man. I walked out and saw him standing in the doorway of the garage. This is my chance. I won't have another. I ran up and shoved him in the back. I heard a crack as he fell down the stairs. I ran down jumped onto both of his arms then stomped his legs. He let out a sharp yell as I dragged him by the back of his shirt deeper into the garage. Now how will I carve this flesh pumpkin? Ah I know what I will do. It is a magic word: evisceration. That's a minimum of 17 points in Scrabble. How it rolls off the tongue nicely.

He was already lying on the ground. His arms and legs were broken so it would be easy. He wouldn't be able to fight back. Now what to use? I stood and thought while I heard screams and curses in the background. I walked upstairs and took a knife from the drawer. It was long and sharp, a handle I could wrap my whole hand around for a good grip. I walked back down the stairs. My father was lying on the ground, tears forming in his eyes. I took a small piece of duct tape and put it over his mouth. I gripped the knife and stabbed his stomach. His eyes grew big with pain

127

and fear. I tore his skin as I ran the knife down to his belly button.

I knew he was dead when I dragged the knife down his chest the first three inches. I took a recycling box and reached my hands into the open flesh, grabbing and tearing out what I think were intestines. I put a fitting top on the box and pushed it into the corner. Then I grabbed the body and dragged it into the same closet where I left my mother. As I opened the door, the first smell that hit me was death— rotting, decaying flesh that the rats had easily found. I pushed my father's body into the closet carelessly and locked the door. I sighed and I walked upstairs, turning off the light and closing the door behind me. Next, I went into the bathroom and thoroughly washed the blood and loose pieces of flesh from my hands.

The sky had darkened, so I put the box of remains on the back of my bike. I slowly pedaled down the street, took a right, then a left, and then stopped at a brick wall up to my knees. I took the box off the back of the bike then poured the stinking remains onto the ground. 'Eat up' is what ran through my mind as bugs and a few rats began to crawl onto the pile of organs on the ground. I got back on my bike and rode home.

* * *

"So that's all that happened?" The figure sitting in the chair looked at me with a serious face.

"Yes." I said.

The man got up from the table and walked over to a filing cabinet, opening it to place papers in, then closing it with a soft clunk.

"Well little girl," he said, as he walked over to the table and sat down. "You're in trouble and I hope you realize that."

All I did was smile and looked at a concrete wall that was where a window would be.

I was driven to a big place that looked like a hospital. When I came in, they told me to strip to my underwear. Once I was naked, they put a "special" jacket on me and walked me down the hallway to a room. The inside was padded and white. There was a bed in the middle of the room along with a chair. They both appeared to be screwed to the ground. When they removed the jacket, they said I would be checked on daily to make sure I was doing alright and if I needed anything to tell them. I sat silently on the floor as the door slammed shut and the lock clicked.

```
Patient: Briggs,Moira
Date secured: 12-3-2013
Secured For:
Psychopathic   behavior
Other: Parents missing,
no other close family,
no other information
known.
Release date: Unknown
```

~~*

Moira Briggs is a teen living in New York's beautiful Hudson Valley. She is a member of her middle school's Creative Writing Club. Moira wrote her first poem at age 3 and is currently working on a novel about the Zombie Apocalypse. Stay tuned !

Outlaw Josie Woot

Larey Batz

Finally, Lucille walked over to his table—well not *exactly* to his table. She stood about eight feet away, pad and pen in hand, contempt in her eyes.

She sighed, her lips pressed to one side. "What ya' having?"

"I've been sitting here for thirty minutes," he said.

"Law says I have ta' serve ya'. Didn't say nothin' 'bout havin' ta' be quick about it."

"You're not that busy, Lucille."

"Packed house 'til you showed up." She glanced at a few of the other customers and her face tightened, making the creases in her wrinkled face deeper. "You eatin' or bitchin'?"

"I'm waiting for someone. I'll just have a coffee for now."

She rolled her eyes. "Who's joinin' ya'? Another rot bag?"

"Why do you have to insult me? I've been a regular customer at this diner for years. We used to talk all the time."

"That was before ya' went and got ya'self initiated. I don't find myself inclined to take up casual conversation with things that wanna eat me."

"How many times do we have to do this? I've had the shots. I don't crave human flesh anymore."

"Ta' hell with those shots. Don't mean nothin'. I know what your kind really wants ta' eat and it ain't on no menu of mine."

"Like I said, cup of coffee for now. And I'd like it from one of the pots behind the counter. None of your 'special blend' from the back, this time please."

The portly waitress flashed a pained smile and walked away. Red's Diner had been his favorite spot in his former life. Coming there, even in his current state, made him feel connected to the person he once was. Even though he was an outcast, he had every right to be there. He was one of the foremost leaders for Zombie rights, and his dream was to see his people integrated at the same rate as had occurred in the major cities. He refused to let his small South Carolina town fall behind the progress made nationally.

After the government contained the outbreak, all remaining zombies were forced to register and undergo 'The Protocol'—a series of injections to eliminate the craving for human flesh and reduce the probability of spreading infection by 99.2 percent. In his small town of Six Ditch, that .8 percentage had become the local rallying cry. T-shirts, bumper stickers, hats and even some versions of the state flag, all carried the slogan 'Remember the 0.8.'

The door chimes caused him to spin around. Unlike the previous five times, the person he was waiting for stepped through the door. Wearing a navy t-shirt and jeans, Agent Annie Walls walked across the floor with quiet confidence and a toothpick riding the corner of her lips. He stood, though in his state, there was little reason to believe she'd have a problem pointing him out.

All eyes followed her as she headed to his booth. She was younger than he imagined from her tone over the phone. Not bad on the eyes. Attractive, but stern features. Long, dark hair. Nice sway in the hips. Not what he was expecting at all, considering she was F.B.I.

After she slid across the worn vinyl, he returned to his seat opposite. "Agent Walls?"

"Bingo." She removed her dark glasses and stared around the diner. "I'm surprised you'd pick this place to meet, Mr. Batz. Are they giving you any flack?"

"No more than the usual. And you can call me Larey."

"Here's the deal, Mr. Batz. My office authorized the tap and we believe she's going out tonight."

"Great. Why don't you arrest her then?"

"We will. But we need to catch her in the act."

Fat fingers slammed a plastic cup on the table and Lucille's arm jerked away a split second later. She took a few steps back and turned toward Agent Walls. "Hmmm. You ain't from 'round here."

Annie tilted her head, eyebrow raised. "What gave me away? My upright posture?"

Lucille parked her hands over her wide hips. "Everybody's a comedian. You ordering or what?"

Annie twisted her lip and glanced across the table at Larey. "Ya' know, I've heard you have a habit of serving some of your customers, coffee with a side of piss, so I think I'll pass."

"Suit ya' self." Lucille's glare turned to Larey. "Make sure you take that cup with ya'."

After she walked away, Larey lifted the lid and dumped a couple of sugar packets inside.

"And she's one of the nice ones," he said, stirring his hot coffee. "So, catching her in the act. Of what? Hunting?"

"This is what I wanted to talk to you about. Currently 'zombie hunting' is a gray area. Could get her ten years. Could get a her a five thousand dollar fine and a wink from the judge. Until the laws are revised, prosecuting people like her is gonna be tricky."

"Five thousand?" He scoffed and took a quick sip. "The way they feel about zombies in this town, they could pass a hat around at a few churches and collect that in an hour. The locals actually consider her a hero, fighting for human rights."

"I know, right? So here's the thing. My office wants to make an example. Something that will make headlines and show we're serious about enforcing these laws. We feel the best way to do that is to catch her in the act of actually killing one of you."

"What?" He almost choked on his last sip. "I'm not doing that."

137

"Mr. Batz, I know how it sounds, but it's the only way to send a real message. She'd get the maximum under the federal statute. Twenty years per kill. Multiple killings would mean life."

"You want me to sacrifice my own kind?"

"No. Not exactly. Just the wanderers. Their brains are too infected to think the Protocol shots will ever bring them back to any real state of consciousness."

"*That's* why we're pushing the government for a cure! If there's hope for me, there's hope for them."

"*You're* ... one of the lucky ones. The newly turned are showing remarkable progress. The older ones, we don't know yet. They could be in that mindless zombie trance forever. Some doctors think it's actually more humane to—"

"To kill them? I've seen some of them get better."

"Really? How many are we talking about? I mean, it's good that they stay to the woods and away from the city until they die off, but I have to be honest. Some people aren't convinced that we should allow them to just roam around like animals in the wild. Some people think they're still dangerous."

"To *who*? The drugs have made them completely passive. They only eat what they find in the woods. Squirrels, snakes, mice. They don't require much to live and when they do feed, it's on animals we consider pests anyway."

"Unfortunately, Mr. Batz, good causes sometimes require martyrs. Their deaths will serve a higher purpose. I believe in your movement and I'm telling you, this is the only way to achieve real progress. Some of your kind will have to die."

He clasped his hands together and stared at her. As much as it pained him to admit, she was probably right. Seeing a human kill a zombie, forcing the country to come face to face with the horrors of its prejudice, might be the only way to rally true support for his cause.

"Fine. Then I'll do it. I'm highly visible in the movement and I'm renewed. My death will do a lot more for publicizing this than a few wanderers."

"No. It can't be you," she said. "You're too important to the cause and my agency considers you a prime asset."

"Well I don't feel comfortable sacrificing one of my own."

"Mr. Batz, she's going out to hunt tonight, regardless of what we do. You asked for our help, this is me helping you. 10 o'clock. Wait for my call."

She slid out of the booth and headed for the door. This time the eyes that watched her, weren't focused on how her jeans hugged her thighs. They were suspicious. They all wanted to know what business *she* could possibly have with *him*—a zombie. The chimes danced and pinged off one another as Annie pushed her way outside. As soon as the door closed, glances shot in Larey's direction. The sounds of throats clearing, faint whispers, and ominous mumbling soon filled the room. He stood, left his money for the coffee, plus tip, and headed for the exit.

***

He met Annie in the rural woods along the outskirts of town. It was where the wanderers gathered at nightfall, staggering around in search of food. They'd become conditioned to waiting until 10PM or later, when most of the town was asleep. Larey looked around, spotting a few wanderers in the distance, their faint growls and moans barely making it to his ears.

He turned to Annie. "Uh, excuse me, but where's your team?"

"Yeah, about that…" She held binoculars to her eyes and scanned the area. "I *am* the team. I sorta lied about having full agency backup on this one."

"Just me and you? Are you crazy? This woman is an expert hunter. We don't stand a chance."

139

"Pipe down, Batz. I've taken out highly organized terrorist cells. I think I can handle one country gal with a gun."

"Why would you come here all the way from D.C., by yourself, to help us?"

"Because I believe in what you're doing. Six Ditch isn't the only place where they still hunt wanderers, but you're one of the few infected that has the balls to speak out about it."

"All I want is for the government to enforce its laws."

"It's gonna take more than laws," she said. "Attitudes have to change. As long as the hunts are just rumors, no one is going to face any real consequence for killing people like you. Too many have lost people they care about, because of fear-mongering and prejudice. We can't afford to just sit on our asses and let ignorance get in the way of helping the infected."

He turned toward her. Her words were laced with a passion he rarely saw from the uninfected, unless it was a politician or a police chief pandering to political correctness. He believed her.

"You lost someone didn't you?"

She lowered the binoculars. "A good friend. He was part of the first wave of infections."

"Was he F.B.I.?"

"No. Civilian. Doctor. A shame he's not here to see ..."

"See what?"

She released a heavy sigh. "This is off the record. I could lose my job for telling you this."

"Tell me."

"The government has a cure. They're just waiting on CDC and FDA approval. They're running trials now."

"Are you serious?"

"That's why I came here. We need to keep as many infected alive as we can."

"Jesus. Why don't they just tell people they have a—
"

"Because what happens if it doesn't work? You think people are going to be patient? The last thing the government needs is for people to start thinking this thing is incurable. 'Close to a cure' is as far as they're willing to go."

"Why me? Why Six Ditch?"

"Like I said. I believe in what you're doing." She looked away. "And..."

"And?"

"You ... you sort of remind me of h—" Her head snapped around. "You hear that?"

Before he could reply, headlights appeared in the darkness. A faded red jeep appeared, and then rolled to a stop at a clearing about fifty yards away. The engine idled for a while before going silent. Two men jumped out of the back with pistols, followed by a woman wearing a mesh hunting cap, and holding a Mossberg shotgun. Under a thin fleece, she wore an oversized football jersey with the number '0.8' on the front. She waved the men forward, and turned her attention to the trees.

While her friends chased after a pack of wanderers roaming across a nearby field, the woman spotted a closer target and headed into the woods. Seconds later, there was a growl, followed by the sound of a shotgun blast and the woman's signature kill celebration—"Woot!"

A minute later, another shot, another celebration.

"What are you waiting for?" Larey asked. "I think this qualifies as 'being in the fucking act'."

"Quiet down. You wanna get us caught?" She tucked the binoculars away and retrieved her sidearm from its holster. "I wasn't counting on her having other people with her. You said she hunted alone."

"This is a disaster."

BANG!

141

"Woot!"

"That came from nearby," she said. "She must be headed our way."

"We need to get the hell out of here."

"I just need to film her in the act." Annie pulled out her phone. "Gonna see if I can sneak up on her."

Larey grabbed her arm. "You're leaving me here?"

She reached inside her jacket pocket, producing a small handgun.

"It's a G41." Annie handed it to him. "It's lightweight, but there's no external safety, so be careful. Do not shoot unless you have to. The last thing you wanna do is draw any unnecessary attention. Just wait for me here. I'll be right back."

Annie crouched and headed off in the direction of the gunfire. Larey sat in the grass behind the trunk of a thick cedar tree, his head pivoting in every direction.

BANG!

"Woot!"

He'd never fired a gun in his former life, so having one in his possession provided little comfort. A few months earlier, he'd rejoiced in finding that sensation had returned to some of his extremities. As the injections worked through his nervous system day by day, he gradually learned to feel things again. Touch, pleasure, pain, all returned in slow increments. The warmth of sunlight was most welcomed. Now, he was experiencing the wind across his face on a cool October night. Yet he was sure the chill in his spine had nothing to do with injections. He was paralyzed with cold fear.

Three shots sounded off in the distance, followed by two more. It wasn't shotgun fire. Sounded like handguns.

Could have been Agent Walls. Could have been the two men.

BANG!

"Woot!"

The woman's voice sounded like it was right behind him. He couldn't stand sitting there waiting to be found so he darted deeper into the woods. He kept low, moving between the trees, keeping eyes and ears open. When he thought he'd heard another 'woot', he spun around waving the gun in the darkness. He looked up and saw an owl perched on a branch.

"Larey!"
He turned around and saw Annie standing next to him, out of breath.
"I thought I told you to stay put," she said.
"I was scared. It sounded like she was right next to me."
"Okay. Calm down."
"I heard shots."
"That was probably me. I took out her friends so it's just her now. I got some good footage, so we need to—"

BANG!

Annie's head exploded right in front of him, showering him in blood and bits of her brain. Meanwhile, her nearly beheaded body thumped the ground and rolled to a stop at his feet. There were strands of her dark hair, still clinging to scattered fragments of skull. When he looked up, he came face to face with a smoking gun barrel, gripped tight by the hands of Outlaw Josie Weiss. Licking her lips, she yanked the sliding pump handle, releasing a

143

spent shell and loading a fresh one. He stared into her rabid eyes, the taste of gunpowder coating his tongue.

"Woot!"

The small Glock by his side felt as if it weighed a ton. It dangled in his fingers as he took a step back.

"Well glory be. If it ain't the leader of the Zombie Rights Movement," Josie said. "This is gonna be my best hunt yet."

"That woman was F.B.I. You just … just killed a Federal Agent. You won't be able to cover that up."

"This is Six Ditch. Ain't no law out here but what we say. By the time they find her body, my granddaughter will be sitting in a rockin' chair with a full head of gray."

"No. They know about you now. I made sure of that. They're gonna come for that woman and they're gonna get you."

"I'm sick of you and your meddling. Trying to integrate. This town is for humans!"

"Is that what you said to your husband before you shot him in the head?"

She shook her head. "That thing wasn't my husband no more. Once he went and got himself bit, he was one of you. Y'all took him from me. I just put him out of his godforsaken misery."

"Look at me," he said. "The injections are working and that agent told me the government has a cure. They're just waiting for it to be approved."

She scoffed. "Lies! Ain't no cure for y'all. Not in this life."

"It is true. You just don't wanna hear it. Because that would mean your husband didn't have to die."

Water formed in her eyes. "He was dead to me the moment your kind got him."

"No. You could have waited ... given him a chance to renew ... like I did. The truth is, it was your black heart that killed him, not the infection."

Tears rolled down her cheeks, trickling past the corners of her quivering lips. "Shut up! Your kind don't belong nowhere but under the dirt! And if the law ain't willing to put you there, I am."

He stared straight ahead, his gaze fixed at a point beyond where she was standing. "I'm not afraid of you."

"Good to know. Thankfully, fear is not required when it comes to dying." She sniffled and raised the shotgun to his eyes. The barrel trembled in her grip. "Head or gut?"

"Head."

She smirked. "That's what I was thinking too. Nice knowin' y—Ommph!!!"

A decaying arm clubbed her over the top of her head, knocking her forward.

BANG!

Her gun exploded just before she lost her grip, sending a wayward shot into the woods. Another blow to the back of her head sent her cap flying and her body to the ground. She rolled over and reached out for the weapon, but a heavy foot pressed her arm in place. The creature growled, drool forming in his mouth and leaking out to splatter her face.

"No! No! Nooooooo!!" She spit the goo from her lips and tried to wrestle free. The monster sat on top of her and pinned her arms back. She watched, horrified as jagged teeth tore into her left shoulder, ripping out a mouthful of flesh and fabric.

While she screamed out in pain, a crowd of wanderer zombies stepped forward from the shadows of the woods. One after the other, they came to watch their apex

145

predator twist and bargain for her life. Soon, she was surrounded by the very menace she wished to exterminate.

"Why?" Her eyes were wide with panic. "Why did it bite me? They ... they don't eat humans anymore! You said the inject—Ahhhhg!"

The creature took another helping from her arm, chewing her bloody tendons before spitting the remains across her jersey, leaving a clump of red meat between the 'o' and the '8'.

"My guess, Ms. Weiss, is that the Zombie-American on top of you at the moment, is one of that .8 percent you and your friends are always crying about. That means you're about to become one of us now."

After flashing its rotted teeth and blackened gums, in what could only be described as an attempted smile, the zombie climbed off of her, growled and walked away. As if sensing the show was over, the rest of the undead gathering parted and disappeared into the woods. Meanwhile, Josie lay on the ground, grimacing at her wounds, frantically trying to slow the bleeding with her hand.

"You son-of-a-bitch! You can't do this to me."

"I didn't."

"You can't leave me here! Take me to the hospital dammit! I need the shots. The injections. I need the cure! You can't leave me!"

Larey picked up the shotgun and walked across the muddy grass until he stood directly over her. "Ain't no cure for your kind. Not in this life anyways."

He placed the end of the barrel flush against her forehead and fumbled around with the pump mechanism until a fresh shell clicked into position.

"No. Please. No! I won't hunt. I'll support your rights. Hell, I'll march for your rights! Please!"

"Now remind me. What's your favorite word again? You know. The one you like shouting after every kill. Oh yeah... I remember now." His finger tightened on the trigger. "I think it goes something like ... Woot!"

Accepting defeat, Josie sighed. "Unwoot."

BANG!

Author and Screenwriter Larey Batz is a native of Memphis TN, but currently resides in Philly, PA. Influenced by writers such as Poe and Langston Hughes, he writes across multiple genres—primarily horror, suspense, sci-fi and dark humor. He is currently finishing "Obey", the sequel to his debut novel "Second Dawn" and has several other projects in the works.

You can follow Larey at:

http://www.facebook.com/lareybatzauthor

http://www.amazon.com/Larey-Batz/e/B00E9EHEMU/

https://twitter.com/LareyBatz

THE END

May all the departed rest in peace.

Made in the USA
Charleston, SC
23 March 2014